BETWEEN DEATH AND A HARD PLACE

A Grey Witch Adventure

JOE WEINBERG

Milton, Ontario

Brain Lag Publishing
Milton, Ontario
http://www.brain-lag.com/

Library and Archives Canada Cataloguing in Publication

Title: Between death and a hard place : a grey witch adventure / Joe Weinberg.
Names: Weinberg, Joe, author.
Identifiers: Canadiana (print) 20220271208 | Canadiana (ebook) 20220271259 | ISBN 9781928011811
  (softcover) | ISBN 9781928011828 (ebook)
Classification: LCC PS3623.E432 B48 2022 | DDC 813/.6—dc23

Content warnings: Death, guns, sex (implied, consensual), violence

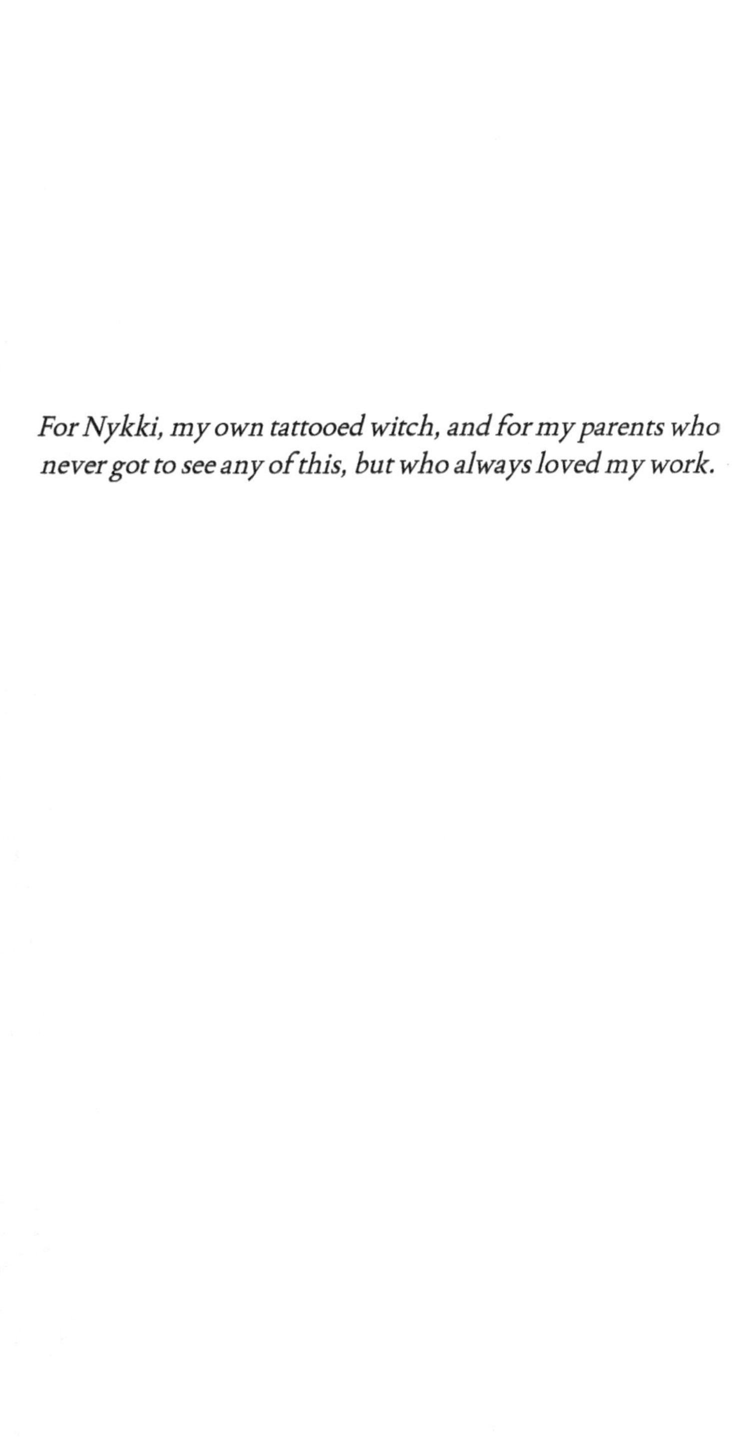

For Nykki, my own tattooed witch, and for my parents who never got to see any of this, but who always loved my work.

CHAPTER ONE

I hope this is just a basic haunting. I really don't want to have to kill anyone.

I focus on my eyes in the rearview mirror. I can lean back and check what I would laughably qualify as makeup, but there's really no point in that. The only thing worth looking at just now is the eyes, because they have to be perfect. They have to be cold glass, reflecting the world without showing anything of the person behind them. They have to be as gray and colorless as my last name. They have to look through people, send that very clear message that I'm not afraid, that I can—and will—kill them all if I have to. The eyes have to be the warning, the bluff that helps me avoid conflicts.

I can't bring my knives inside, which makes the bluff a bit more necessary. But I still have me, I still have my body, my wits, and my ink. So there's still some backup to the bluff that I can call on if I have to. But the eyes will sell it, and if they sell it right, then there won't really be a need to prove that my bite is almost as bad as my bark.

I slam the car door a little harder than I probably have to. I press the key fob to lock the doors, then lift away the piece of hematite that stops the spell circuit from completing, activating my own special brand of alarm. Other people want car alarms that make lots of noise and supposedly scare off potential thieves, but more likely just annoy the sleeping people within earshot. I want an alarm that makes people look past my shitty car and on to better and easier options, forgetting what they saw and dismissing my car as completely unimportant. It's not quite invisibility (that would be more expensive), but it gets close enough that it has the same purpose.

I found parking in downtown Minneapolis, and that in itself is an accomplishment. The last thing I need is for people to look at my car and decide they want to actually do something about my accomplishment. I've never had my car broken in to—Hennepin is pretty brightly lit at night, between the Gay 90s and First Ave, Crave and Fogo de Chao, there's always a lot of light and a decent crowd of people. I'm not saying that there isn't any crime—it's a city, after all—but it's a relatively safe neighborhood. At least, for cars. Cars with magic that makes people ignore them, anyway. Okay, maybe a bad example.

I take a deep breath and let my coat spread out a bit after being crumpled by me sitting on it. I have to wrap it around like a skirt before I get in the car or some of it gets stuck in the door and either drags along the ground, or just makes me feel like an idiot when I realize it. The trench coat isn't the warmest thing in the world, but it looks like it could be, and in Minneapolis, that's all I really care about. Temperature itself has never been an issue for me.

I can see the bright lights of the Gay 90s in the distance, but that's not where I'm headed. Not tonight. Tonight is all about Club Trinity. Which, granted, is right down the street, not even a block away. Walking to the door of Trinity, I see a bouncer I recognize. What's his name? Carter? Collin? Carl? No. Oh, right. "Hey Charlie," I say, walking past the line and right up to the door.

"AJ," he says with a slight nod and a frown. "Do I need to

search you?"

"I'm not packing weapons," I say. "Just here to talk."

He scoffs. "I'll believe that one when I see it," he says. "Look, just try not to make too much of a mess, okay? I like the new set of chairs. Management finally picked something comfortable, and I don't want to have to wait another ten years before they get lucky again."

Holding up my hand, I make the boyscout salute. Don't ask why. "I solemnly swear I will not break a chair over anyone, Charlie. I'll do my best to keep them all intact."

He nods and gestures over his shoulder for me to go in, not even asking me for the cover. "If you want to smash the candle holders on the table though, feel free," he says as I pass. "They're so seventies kitsch it hurts my delicate artistic sensibilities."

I pat Charlie on the shoulder and laugh as I walk by. Patting him on the shoulder is no easy task. I'm not short, but Charlie is like a mountain. Easily seven feet tall and twice as wide across as I am, the man looks like he could pick me up and rip me in half like a phone book. So of course, everyone assumes he's this big dumb thug. None of them ever ask him about fashion or design decisions, or about what lighting works best. Which is a shame, for them. Charlie's the one who told me to get this coat instead of the white one. Said this one brought out my eyes more, and made me look more dangerous, especially with the frock.

He also tried to get me to buy oxblood colored boots, but I can only handle so much fashion advice.

The music inside isn't so loud as to be offensive, but maybe that's just because the song is only just starting. It's the Cure, that lullaby song about the spider wanting to eat people. Not portentous at all. The dance floor is almost empty, save for the few fixtures, the dancers who are either so high they can't hear the music anyway, or those so lost in their heads and the movement that they don't care what plays, so long as it's not Bieber.

Most of the crowd, though, is sitting around at tables, having drinks, catching breathers, or engaging in deep conversations. There's laughter every so often. Some of it has humor, but most is lined with vitriol and bile, that dark mocking laughter that anyone who was ever picked on as a kid can remember.

Most people weren't laughed at because they were the bald girl from that other school—*I hear she murdered her boyfriend— what a freak...* but hey, we can't all be as lucky as I am.

Wearing gray makes me almost look colorful in here. The color scheme is so monochromatic it looks like an art film in black and white. White skin, black lips, black clothes, black fingernails. The girls aren't that much better. Every so often there's a slash of red, enough to make people think about blood without having to smell the stuff.

I head up to the bar and slide across a stool, leaving my coat hanging behind me. The bartender comes bouncing over, her T-shirt clipped tight behind her to make it that much easier for men to make out the shape of her 'tip makers,' as she calls them. She has a smile on her face, one that always seems to be there when she's working. She once told me it was because the rubber floor mats she walks across actually make her feel like she's working in a bouncy castle. And everyone has to smile when they're in a bouncy castle. It's like a rule of the universe or something.

"Hey AJ!" she says, slapping her hands on the bar top, partially to make noise and partially to stop herself from bouncing past. "Ooh, you're wearing your work coat." The smile slips away from her eyes, but remains plastered on her face. "Something I should be worried about?"

While it's true that I am working tonight, I'm not doing *that* kind of work. The violent type that tends to disrupt businesses, start fires, and make bouncers wary of me; I'm not here for any of that tonight. I'm here on a simple recon mission. Just supposed to check the place out, see if the various egghead precog types were right about me needing to be here. I'm just looking for a ghost that, hopefully, is still mentally intact. I'm not here for violence.

I hope.

I shake my head. "No need to worry, Gina. Fucking hell, between you and Charlie, you'd think I was some kind of walking natural disaster or something."

She shrugs. "If the boots fit," she says.

"Look, that was *one* time. And I said I was sorry. Even got the ban lifted and everything."

She smirks at that. We both know how much more getting that ban lifted was because of her than of me. "You want a drink?" she asks.

"Give me a Melon Ball," I say. "Extra sweet."

She heads off to get the vodka, midori, and the orange juice, adding a touch of pineapple juice to the mixture to make it sweet enough that most people won't be able to taste the booze in the first place.

As she's making the drink, I spin my stool and lean back against the bar, taking the place in. It's a pretty simple crowd tonight. I tuck some hair behind my ear, exposing a septagram tattoo and with it, the magical overlay of the room. As I thought, most of them are human, just your average workaday goths coming to blow off some steam on a Tuesday night. And like always, where there are goths there are vampires, but just two of them that I can see, which is more on the low end than the high. And looking at them, it seems like they're hanging out in crowds that recognize them, which means they're careful when they feed. And therefore not my problem.

Out on the dance floor, I can see my client. Or at least, the reason I assume I got called here. Not for violence; that's a plus. I look at her and wonder what her deal is. She wasn't there before, but then, she isn't really there now. It's just the projection, the aura of her spirit left behind when she died. She's going about her life as best she can, at least the parts of it that matter to her.

It's not living, but it's as close as she can get to it now. It's something that will keep her sane, relatively speaking, until her issues get resolved or she loses it completely.

I don't want to interrupt her. If she can still hold on to her life strongly enough to dress the part of the club, I want her to keep doing it. I want her to stay strong for as long as possible. Besides, the longer she looks the way she did in life, the more likely I'll be able to figure out what's tying her here.

Ghosts get tied down by a lot of things. Some kind of passion, certainly. Also locations, personal items, even people. Most hauntings happen because the ghost is tied to a place, and has probably lost any real comprehension of what happened. It's not that ghosts don't know they're dead—I mean, that happens sometimes, but usually it's the other way. They don't think that they're alive, they just forget that they're dead. And once that happens, all bets are off. Frustration starts to build, which brings anger, which eventually starts to bring violence.

I get called in for those sorts of situations too, thanks to the ink on my fingers, but it's pretty clear that she isn't looking to start any trouble.

This one doesn't have any of the signs, at least not right off the bat. She's dancing to Burn by Nine Inch Nails, which is the song currently playing, so she's still interacting with the world as if she were a part of it. But she's not trying to make eye contact with anyone or get their attention. She's moving away from them as they get closer to her, and she seems completely without any concern of being watched or judged. Maybe she was like that in life, maybe she just knows that they can't see her and is dancing like no one is watching. Because, as far as she knows, no one is. No one can.

There's a glint of light from something on her chest. Probably a necklace of some sort, likely one of the items that ties her to this world. If I need to just get rid of her, I just have to get rid of her ties. Then she'll fall away to wherever it is the dead go when they're really gone.

That's one way to play this. Or I could help her settle whatever it is that's keeping her here. Then she can move on of her own free will, which I imagine is probably better for her. I don't know though—I've never died myself. What really matters is that I settle her, one way or another, before a necromancer finds the ties that bind her and uses them to control her. A ghost being controlled tends to get angry and frustrated a whole lot faster. Worse, they tend to want revenge against the person controlling them. That's all well and good if they can escape. But if not, or if the necromancer disappears, they may just decide to go after those who look like the necromancer. Or, you know, all men between the ages of eighteen and forty. That's when ghosts go bad, when they become specters. That's when they get really dangerous.

Hopefully, I can avoid that happening to her. But first, I need to talk to her. Which in itself presents all kinds of problems. I can see her; she's part of the magic in the area now, so with my septagram uncovered, I can see her just fine. But I can't *hear* her. When she talks, I won't know what she's saying unless I can read lips. Maybe I'll get lucky and she'll know sign language. But given that she's dancing to actual music playing, and seems to be pretty solidly on beat, I'm pretty sure she isn't deaf. Which makes sign unlikely.

Well, no one ever said being a witch was easy.

I don't really have a plan for how to get her attention, either. For right now, I'm just watching her. Maybe she'll feel my eyes on her and come over to check me out. Maybe she'll look up and realize that, unlike everyone else in here, I can actually see her. Or maybe she'll ignore me like she's ignoring everyone else. And then what? How do you get a ghost's attention?

Gina comes back with my drink, and I turn back to the bar, my hair falling forward and covering the septagram. She glances up at my hair line and smiles knowingly. "Seeing someone?" she asks. Anyone overhearing might think it a perfectly innocuous question. Gina's great at those.

I nod. "One of the dancers," I say.

"What's she look like?"

"Maybe five four, somewhere around a buck, buck ten. Straight black hair with a—" I hold my hand up to my own chocolate brown hair, "streak of blue. Some kind of necklace, I couldn't make it out. Boots to her knees, heels not platforms."

Gina nods. "That sounds like about ninety percent of the girls in here, and maybe half the boys," she says. "Still, that's a bit on the short side. Any piercings?"

"Nose, eyebrow, snake fangs, and ears, that I could see. Oh, and a teardrop on the right."

Gina lets out a sigh that tells me I've hit gold. "That would be Michelle. I was afraid something might have happened to her. She's a regular, but it's been about a week since she was in here."

"Regular as in every night?"

"Tuesdays, Thursdays, and Saturdays," Gina says. "Goth, punk, and industrial."

I nod. "That sounds about right. When was the last time she was here?"

"Saturday before last. This is the second Tuesday she's missed. Or, I guess, hasn't missed." She smiles a little, but it's a sad smile. "Does she know you can see her?"

I shake my head and take a sip of my Melon Ball. Yeah, that's sweet. Really sweet. My body loves it, and I end up drinking nearly a third of it in one go. I'd keep going, but I may still need to drive tonight. Odds are, I can't just sit down and talk with Michelle. I didn't even bring a Ouija board.

Those piss me off, by the way. Not because they work (they don't), but because people think that they're this ancient thing, when really they were invented by Parker Brothers. But they can be useful when talking to someone you can see but can't hear. She could point at the letters and spell out a word. It would take forever, but it would be a way of communicating.

Or she could know sign language. I took the time to learn it. Why can't the dead?

"She seems to know that no one can see her," I say. "Enough that she isn't bothering to check if people are watching her. I guess I could wave at her or something." Yeah, because that won't make me look like an idiot, waving at empty space.

"You could always go and bump into her on the dance floor."

I guess I could do that. Thanks to the tattoos on my fingers, I can make contact with the insubstantial. I mean, I can actually touch her as if she's solid. Which might freak her out, or make her think I'm like her. But she's been making it a point to move away from anyone who dances too close to her. There's no way I could pull off an accidental collision.

On the other hand, that might not be a bad thing. I shrug out of my coat and leave it on the stool. "Keep an eye on that for me?" I ask Gina, taking another long 'sip' from the Melon Ball.

She nods. "Absolutely. Wouldn't want someone touching it and bursting into flames."

I roll my eyes. "One time," I mutter under my breath, heading out towards the dance floor.

I put my hair up in a ponytail with a band from my wrist, making sure to free the septagram and overlay the magic in the area. I may look a bit out of place on this dance floor, wearing just a black tank top and matching jeans with the cuffs rolled up to the top of my boots. But I'm less out of place here than I would be in most dance clubs. I at least have the right colors on. And my bare arms are so covered with ink that virtually anything I'm wearing gets its own hard core cred.

What they'll be able to see, especially in the lighting of the club, is just swirls of black down my arms. They start as arrows from my shoulders, then kind of dissolve into a tentacle like design. There isn't much detail, but that was the point. That tattoo is there to cover the others. The others that are various glyphs, symbols, runes, and pictographic spells, things that would hurt the human eye to look at for too long. I should know; putting them there gave me a migraine every fucking time.

Plus there's the pain. People who have tattoos will tell you the pain isn't that bad. And it's not; it's like having a cat scratch at you for a really long time. It'll hurt, but it's no big deal. That's with a tattoo gun. That's a normal tattoo.

These spells in my skin were stabbed in by hand. It feels like dripping battery acid on the skin. You never get used to it. It never hurts any less. And once you start, you can't stop until you're done. Otherwise, you have a wasted half spell that doesn't do a fucking thing, and you went through that pain for nothing. You can't just finish it later, either. You have to start all over again.

Covering them up was much easier. That I could do without really paying all that much attention, just shading for some contours and making sure the lines are crisp. Doesn't matter that they go over and through the real things. Those spells were designed to work even when covered. Not like the septagram. Same process, different results.

I dance out onto the floor, moving my hands in a gentle wave that passes up my arms to my shoulders, a movement that makes it look like I have no bones when I do it right. I pay a lot of attention to my hands, making sure they stay pointed and outstretched. I took a belly dancing class once, for a couple of weeks, and they told me that the poise of the hand is as important as everything else. They were really big on the whole thing of using different muscles independently of one another. That's why I wanted to learn. It's also why I ended up quitting while I could still feel those muscles.

The result has made my dancing almost serpentine, flowing along like the chords of a Voltaire song. It can be distracting to some, but usually it just gets me ignored in a goth club. The rest of my body doesn't move the same way as my hands. I move my hips like a dancer, another remnant from the classes, but I move my feet like a fighter. I keep my balance steady, I keep my shoulders straight, and I don't cross my legs, not ever. Those who really know have told me that my dancing looks like my arms are trying to relax while the rest of my body stands around it with suits, sunglasses, and a little radio in the ear, just waiting for a threat so they can usher me off to Air Force One or something.

Okay, so I'm not a great dancer. Certainly not as good as the girl I'm slowly moving towards. She moves like she really has no bones, like she's not from this planet. Her hips are moving the way the girl who tried to teach me moved, and her feet and legs move with a grace that make her combat boots look out of place. My combat boots look appropriate. She looks like she's a ballerina dressed up to scare off high school boys. She sways her entire body, and it seriously looks like she has had her spine segmented. No one should be able to move that way. I'd be a bit worried if I hadn't seen it before. It's a trick of the movement, of the control she has, or had, over her body. She can move her lower body while keeping her head perfectly still. That's how it looks. But really, she's moving everything, she's just negating the movement with her head, moving in the opposite directions of her body so it *looks* like her head is keeping still.

It's a skill I never mastered. But she looks like she was a real dancer. Maybe even a professional. She's got the muscle tone for it. Though looking closely, she doesn't have the age for it. This isn't a girl who got into the club to drink, unless she had a fake ID. This is a girl who was just here to dance. That also might explain why she's so good at it.

I slide towards her, extending my hands out to my sides and then turning to face her full on. I don't want her to panic, but I need her to know that I can see her. I try locking eyes with her, but her eyes are closed. She's lost in the music, lost in the dulcet tones of Trent Reznor, back before he started making music for

Gen Z.

Plan B then. I make a sliding step towards her, my feet moving into position to throw some seriously nasty knees in her direction. Then I bend forward and bring my hands down slowly, waving them around.

And sliding them down her arm.

Anyone watching will think it was just a bit of a stretch for me, like I'm trying to show off. But they can't see her. She opens her eyes in absolute shock and looks at me. I smile and wink at her.

She starts to talk, but I can't hear her. I can see magic, I can't hear it. I'm not a necromancer, and I'm not a medium. That magic is beyond me, largely because of all the other magic I have inked into my skin; it doesn't leave enough leaking out to be able to talk to the dead, and I've never had the desire or the need to add a tattoo to one of my ears so I could hear them. I can't really communicate with her. But I can see her, and that might be enough.

I walk off the dance floor, looking back at her and raising my eyebrows as I go. As I'd hoped, she follows after me, so intent on me that she literally walks right through someone else coming to dance to the Rammstein song starting as I go to a table away from the bar.

She sits down across from me and starts talking. From what I can see, she's going a mile a minute, and I can't hear word one.

I hold up my hands. "Hold on," I say. "Can you hear me?"

She says something. I'm guessing it was somewhere along the line of, "Of course I can hear you. Can't you hear me?"

"I can't hear you," I say, shaking my head. "I can only see you." I flash her a few basic signs with my hands, but she looks at it like I'm signing in Greek. And I'm not. It just means she doesn't sign. Long shot anyway.

She tries to pantomime a pen and paper. I shake my head. "You won't be able to hold the pen," I say. "And before you ask, I am not using a Ouija board like a bored sorority girl."

She laughs at that. I wish I could hear it. From the way it lights up her face, she seems like her laugh would be infectious. "Okay. I'm sorry we can't get more complex than this for now, but I'm going to ask you questions, and you nod your head for yes, shake your head for no. Okay?"

She nods and gives me the thumbs up. She's probably just happy to be able to communicate at all, despite how annoying this has got to be.

"Do you know what happened to you?" I ask.

She nods.

"Do you know why no one can see you?"

She nods again. Okay, good. That means she knows she's dead. And she's not in denial about it. That helps. Usually, when the dead don't know they're dead, they get angry and frustrated. A normal situation for a normal person, but the rules are different for ghosts.

"Is there a message you need to give someone?"

She shakes her head. Of course it wouldn't be that easy.

"Are you looking for revenge?"

Shakes her head again. Also good; the vengeful spirits tend to go bad fast. But what else could it be? If she's not here to send a message, and not here to get revenge, what's left? She can't want to warn someone of something; that's back to the message. Does she want to finish up an art project? See the next Star Wars movie? No, it has to be something important.

"Is there something that you have to finish?"

She nods. Maybe it *is* Star Wars.

"Can you show me?"

She fingers the necklace I saw light glinting off of before. It's a crucifix. Not a gothic one. She has one of those too, and an ankh and all the other stereotype jewelry that tells me she was just a normal girl. But that crucifix, simple and silver and elegant, that's something different. That's something that matters to her.

"Can you show me what you need to finish?" I ask.

She nods, still playing with the little cross.

I sigh. "Okay," I say. "Come on, show me where we have to go."

She nods and starts to get up, then falls back to the chair as if jerked off her feet. She looks at me, scared, and says something. She grabs the cross, and I can see her jolt off to the side several feet. But it's not like she's moving. It's like she's being moved. And being moved by the cross itself.

Which can only mean one thing.

"Shit," I say. "Okay. Hold it together," I tell her. "I'll find you. Don't let go, don't forget what you need." She screams, but I can't hear it. "And whatever happens," I grab her hand and force her to look at me. "Remember that it's not your choice. You're being forced to do it. It's not your fault."

She looks at me in confusion, then is tugged away from me so hard that it nearly pulls me off my feet. When I look for her, she's gone. But I knew she would be.

I head back to the bar and finish my drink in one swift gulp, gathering my jacket and throwing money on the bar.

"What's wrong?" Gina asks me.

"Someone got her," I say.

"You mean?"

I nod. "Necromancer."

INTERLUDE ONE

It was like something out of a movie. Sophomore year of high school, the mousy girl who developed over the summer, still not quite used to her new body. The popular boy, a year older than her. Dating for a few months, about to go to prom together. Only she wants to lose her virginity before the dance. She wants to get it out of the way.

He is gentle. He is careful. He cares about her, and she cares about him. There's Blues Traveler playing on his tape deck. Back when there were still tape decks. John Popper crooning about his Canadian Rose, heavy breathing, the smell of sweat and the giggling as they try to find a good position for him to enter her. She bites her lip, wondering if it will hurt, having been told it would, warned that there would be blood, but unsure what would happen. Him trying to act manly and in control, like he knows what he is doing when he is just as clueless as she is. Young love, young lust.

He uses all the moves he's learned from pornography he's watched. She keeps her hand down there to help guide him in, and because it feels good. They grind against each other, giggling when they make noises. He keeps asking her if she is okay, because he's one of the good guys. He doesn't force her, and he really would stop if she said anything.

But she doesn't say anything. And they keep moving together, "Business as Usual" playing on the tape. If they noticed the song, they would have laughed, but they're too focused on each other. Too wrapped up in their own pleasure.

Then she starts feeling warm. Hot. She thinks it's part of the process, and she begins to moan and make noises like the women in the pornography *she's* watched. Her sounds push him over the edge, and he thinks they are orgasming at the same time.

It's his last thought.

A few seconds later, she shivers and looks around. The music has stopped; they never made it to "Yours". And she'd never listen to that album again. The car is gone. Her clothes are gone. Her hair is gone. He is gone.

Like a movie. But not a romance.

CHAPTER TWO

Rushing outside and looking for a trail normally wouldn't help. The problem with cities is that there's so much magic going on, so many trails, that there's usually no way to reliably follow one. But there is one kind of magic that is both territorial and rare enough to be able to follow, at least for a little while: necromancy.

I can see a strain of necromantic magic; every brand of magic has its own particular scent, its own feel. A color, almost. But there's a lot of that around here. Goth clubs. Vampires. Anything undead gives off that magic to at least a small extent. There's a rush of it across the bridge, probably over by Ground Zero. Plus some weird things coming from Nicollet Island (but there always are). So just looking for magic, even for death magic, isn't a good idea, but it's the best I've got.

Maybe I can follow the strongest concentration of it. Maybe the trail will lead me to the girl. Maybe it will lead me to a coven of necromancers just waiting for the opportunity to sacrifice a witch with magic bound into her flesh. That would be just my luck.

But the options are to either go chasing after the only lead I've got, or let that girl become the slave to some unscrupulous asshole who thinks fucking with the dead sounds like a really neat idea. So I follow.

There's no time to stop at the car and get my gear. Magic trails do dissipate, and the further away I get from the club, the faster it's going to fade. Magic only stays in place when there's a lot of it. Whatever spell is pulling her towards the fetter object, towards the necromancer, it's not a super strong spell, so it doesn't leave much of a trail. It's fading away almost as fast as it's forming. I wish I could explain it. But I can't; too busy running.

My feet don't pound against the pavement. Unless I'm holding still, I don't really weigh enough to do that. As I move, most of my weight is taken into the air. Not quite flying, and probably not quite enough for me to run across a pool of water, but enough that I don't get shin splints and I can run a hell of a lot longer than most people. I do a half marathon three times a week. And I run in almost absolute silence, the ripple of my coat in the wind louder than the sound of my footsteps. Useful for hunting things down, useful for running through the streets of Minneapolis.

I weave through the sparse crowds on the street, barely looking at people. I sprint through traffic, dodging a car and wincing at the noise of the honking horn. But I can't afford to wait for the light to change. I have to keep running, and pretend those screams about a crazy bitch are referring to someone else.

I race across the First Street bridge and over to the Riverview area. During the day, it's a nice area. There's a movie theater, the road is kind of cobblestone like, and there's a great sushi place. There are offices and shit too, but I really only care about the movies and the sushi. Lots of times, when there are big street festivals (like Pride), the road is lined with booths. It's a great place, during the day.

At night, especially this late, it's one of the worst possible places to be. The bridge goes overhead, leaving a lot of dark areas where things can go bump all night long. The restaurants are closed, and this late, so is the theater. The streetlights only project enough light to pretend you can see, not enough to actually protect you, and the grass muffles noise with surprising effectiveness, especially under the bridge.

At night, this is one of the worst possible places to be in Minneapolis. Okay, that's not the worst place as far as most people are concerned. I'm not going to get jumped by a gang here, or shot by a cop who mistakes me for an innocent young black man (too soon?), but there are worse things here in the dark. No humans around this area at this time means it's free rein for the things to go bump in the night. There are yuppie neighborhoods nearby, but they're all far enough away not to matter, but close enough that no one suspects anything bad will happen here. Making it the perfect place for terrible things that don't want to get seen to happen.

Any human who *does* come out here at night isn't all that likely to make it home in one piece. There's a word for humans who come out here. It's not 'stupid,' either.

It's 'snack.'

The trail leads under the bridge, to one of the little alcoves that during the day seems like a fun place to take pictures that look like there are vampires there, but during the night seem like a fun place for vampires to *actually hang out*. I run in before I really think about what I'm doing. So I end up charging, unarmed, into the den of a necromancer who has literally just finished a ritual to bind a spirit to his will. And a fresh spirit, one strong enough to hold on to most of her life.

If I had a knife, I could probably kill him without much effort. The space is pretty open, and there's only about forty feet between him and me. I could cut that distance pretty quick and throw the knife before he knew what was going on. But no, I had to be unarmed to go into the club, and that means I had to chase this whole thing down without a weapon. Which means all I've got are my fists and my wits.

The odds could be worse. Probably.

"Who are you?" he asks.

I roll my eyes at the sound of his voice. He can't be older than twenty. Actually, twenty might be pushing it. He's just some punk kid trying things way beyond his pay grade. I'm kinda glad I didn't kill him. There might be a chance for redemption for him. How did a kid this young get the kind of magical moxie necessary for binding a spirit?

"I'm the one unhappy that you're binding spirits to your will," I say, taking a few steps towards him as I catch my breath. I reach into a pocket and pull out my 'badge.' To most people, it looks like a piece of blank cardboard, about the size of a small playing card. To those who can *see*, it's way more.

"Don't come any closer!" he says. I would have ignored him, but he raises up something in his hand that I can't see and it makes a very special clicking noise. The clicking noise of a hammer being pulled back on a pistol.

There's a lot I can handle. A gun shot isn't one of them.

I put my hands up and stop walking. "A gun? Seriously?"

He looks at me, at the card in my hand, but doesn't seem to understand what it is. So either he can't see it, or he just doesn't know. Too new. Another point in the weird column; no one who can bind a spirit from across town should be that new.

I sigh. "Does no one respect the game anymore?"

His hand is shaking, but not enough. He moves the gun down a little and tilts his head to the side. I'm still too far away. "What?" he asks.

"You're an evil necromancer," I say. "You're supposed to be cackling about your plan being complete, or about your triumph being inevitable, or whatever other cliché you care to name. You should be scoffing at me, not even considering me the slightest threat. Send your minions after me, you know? But no, you had to go and get a fucking gun. That takes all the drama out of it, don't you think?"

"Drama?" he asks. "You think this—what the fuck is *wrong* with you?"

I shrug. "Combination of poor impulse control, violent temperament, and strong magical lineage, I'm told."

"Seriously? You have an answer? Who does that?"

"Look, buddy, I'm supposed to be the one upset that things aren't going according to cliché. You don't get to take that. That's my thing."

"Who the fuck are you?"

"I'm AJ," I say. "And I'm here for the girl you just bound."

"The girl I just—you're here for Michelle?"

I nod. I guess that *was* her real name. Probably didn't bother with a fake ID, which means she wasn't a drinker. Or at least that she had some respect for the law. A good girl. "I want her cross."

"Well you can't have it," he says. "I won't let you take her."

Okay, something is clearly wrong here. This doesn't sound like your typical evil necromancer plot. Maybe there's a happy ending here. Maybe this is a star-crossed lovers thing, and he just wants to bind her so that no one else can, so they can be together forever. Some kind of twisted necromantic suicide pact.

"Is—is Michelle your girlfriend?" I ask.

He shakes his head. "N-no. Not yet." He takes a deep breath, stands a bit straighter. "But she will be. She'll learn to love me."

Or it could be a creepy kid who finally finds a magical loophole to get the girl he was too afraid would reject him. Bind her spirit, get power over her actions, and make her at least pretend to like you. More than a little bit rape-y. Any pity I had for the kid dissolves pretty fucking fast.

"Ew," I say. I take a few steps closer.

He raises the gun again, holding it steady in both hands. "Don't come any closer!" he says. "I will shoot you."

I wonder if I could try the whole 'safety is on' gambit with him. He looks nervous, or at least sweaty. Then again, it's such an obvious ploy.

I lower my hands and put them in my pockets, returning my card/badge somewhere safe, and take as nonchalant a pose as I can while someone points a gun at me. "Suit yourself," I say. "I can wait for backup."

"B-backup? You're not a cop."

"I know. I really don't look like one, do I?" I smile. "All the tats, the smell of smoke. No one would ever suspect me of being undercover, would they?"

"Show me your badge."

I laugh. After all, I already did. Or tried to, anyway. He didn't recognize it. "Did you know that if you ask someone if they're a cop, they don't *actually* have to tell you? Who in their right mind would go under cover and bring a badge with them?"

"I haven't broken any laws," he says. "I didn't kill her."

"I know," I say. "But you are pointing a gun at me."

"You were going to attack me." Fair point.

"I'm sure they'll take your word over mine."

"You can't prove I was doing magic."

I laugh. "So what? You have a gun. I don't. What kind of reaction do you think backup would have in those circumstances?" I take one hand and tap it against my lip. "Do you think they'll ask you to drop it, or would they just shoot you? You know, to be safe. Wouldn't want to risk my life, would they?"

He's starting to look panicked. I love it when they're gullible. I probably could have told him the safety was on after all. Of course, he might have just pulled the trigger to find out if that was true, and then I'd end up shot; it's very high on my to-do list *not* to end up shot.

"Or you could put the gun down," I say, "and we can just be two people talking."

He holds his other hand out. A little nimbus of flame appears around his hand. "I can burn you to a crisp before you get any closer," he says.

I smile. "All the more reason not to need the gun, right?" I hold my arms out wide, to show that I'm unarmed. I even take off my coat and let it drop to the floor, so he can see I'm not a threat. Well, to make him think I'm not. My magic may not be showy, but it's there and it's strong enough that I'm not even a little worried about him trying to burn me to a crisp. All I'm worried about is the gun.

He uncocks the gun and lowers it.

"Put it down," I say, trying to keep my voice steady. "It's just for show anyway."

The gun falls from his fingers, taking away the only real threat.

I rush him.

He's true to his word, and flame shoots out of his hand, slamming into my chest with the heat of an inferno. My shirt doesn't stand a chance.

It only takes one swing across the face to drop him unconscious.

I look down at myself, topless but unharmed. Fire can't hurt me anymore. Fire was my first element. I nudge him with my foot and he groans. "Bitch," I say. "These are probably the first tits you've ever seen. Pity you didn't take the time to enjoy them."

I pull out a sharpie from my pocket, thankful that the fire didn't melt my pants or anything in my pockets, and pull off my belt. I draw binding runes along the leather, checking every so often to make sure he isn't heading back towards consciousness. Once it's done, I infuse a bit of energy into it—I can't really manage much, but it'll work—then I tie his ankles and wrists.

I move my hair away from the septagram and look at him. There's a lot of power thrumming through him, but the belt is binding him pretty well, for now at least. He won't be able to sling any magic around when he wakes up, at least not until the spells on the belt dissipate. There's one weird thing—a pulsing sort of strand that is pulling away from him, like it detached from the back of his neck and is just dissolving. I don't get a good enough look to really see what it is, other than weird and disconcerting. It's gone now, and I guess that's all that matters. I try to follow it, but it's too fast. I do see an odd sigil on the wall that also seems to be fading.

I walk closer and take a look at the symbols. I'm not really sure what the spell is, but I might be able to figure it out.

There's a glyph for location; easy enough to figure out. Then gathering, reaping, and death. Interesting combination. The reaping here is meant to refer to crops, but with death thrown in on top, it kind of has a grim reaper vibe. What's particularly weird is that the spell, whatever it was, didn't go off. And more to the point, it's already starting to fade away. Like it was here to react to something, but that thing never happened. All in all, it's not *that* complex of a spell, but the way it's put together doesn't quite make sense to me. Like it's a kind of magic that I just don't understand. Which is weird; there aren't many of those.

I look down at the kid. Was the spell here to collect my life energy when he killed me? Or was it to collect his when I killed him? Either way, how the fuck did someone know to put it there? That shouldn't be possible. I'd ask the kid, but I don't think he really knows.

He gives a groan behind me; I need to make sure he isn't waking up yet.

He won't wake up comfortable, and he won't wake up able to do all that much. Maybe he'll get off light. Probably not. That wasn't normal fire he flung at me, and he broke some pretty serious laws doing it. If all he'd done was bind Michelle, there'd be a chance. But throw in the attack on me, particularly the use of soul fire, and the future does not look good—or long—for him.

I press the speed dial on my cell. As soon as the line connects, I say, "Confirmed necromancer in violation of the law. Binding unwilling spirits, using soul fire to assault and resist arrest.

Current location."

Then I hang up and start looking through the kid's pockets until I find the cross I saw the girl—Michelle—was wearing in the club. I hold it out in my hand, palm flat, and whisper her name.

She comes into view after a few seconds, quite a bit less substantial than before. She looks tired, drained. At least I know where the soul fire came from. "Michelle?" I say. She nods. "You're bound to this necklace. I can unbind you, but it will send you on with whatever you had unfinished."

She looks sad, almost defeated.

Damn it. I'm such a sucker. "Or I can hold onto this and help you finish whatever it was you were trying to finish, then you can move on all on your own."

She smiles at that, and I sigh, slipping the necklace around my own neck.

"Now," I say to myself, "all I need to do is get back to my car or my apartment without anyone noticing that I'm completely topless." I sigh.

"I really need an asbestos bra."

INTERLUDE TWO

The next thing she remembers is someone putting a bracelet on her, clicking closed, but not like a handcuff. She wants it to feel like a handcuff. She deserves that. Geoff is dead, and it's her fault. Entirely her fault.

She stands when the judge comes in, settling into her seat when given permission. Her hair has started to grow back. His parents are in the courtroom, but she can't look at them. She can't look at anyone without crying.

There's a lot of crying.

The judge rules that it was an accidental expression of magical power. It's not hard to prove; she's never shown any inclination to power. While her parents both have the genes, neither one is a practitioner. She is the eldest child, so there was no warning, no expectation that she would need training.

She is found not guilty.

But he's still dead.

CHAPTER THREE

I wrapped my coat around myself to cover up with, and was on my third cigarette before backup actually showed up. Good thing he didn't call my bluff, I guess. It's another twenty minutes before they've secured him in better anti-magic cuffs and take the time to give me back my belt. I smudged the symbols, breaking the tiny enchantment I'd put on it, before putting it back on. The last thing I wanted was a belt I couldn't take off. Never mind how frustrating that would be for my social life, it would mean that I couldn't even change my pants. And that's just gross.

The debrief was pretty simple. I had the guy dead to rights. He'd bound a spirit *and* drained it to power other magics. Pretty solid no-nos no matter who you are. Open and shut case.

Only it's not. The shit this kid was doing was not first-day-on-the-job necromancy. It wasn't the kind of thing you just accidentally figure out how to do. But it was clear that he didn't know what he was doing, not really. He wasn't in control of himself, didn't have the kind of training you normally expect someone to have before they start that kind of exercise of power. This kid was, at best, an apprentice of some sort. He shouldn't have had the knowledge, let alone the willingness, to do what he did to Michelle. Not for years. And then there's the power involved, way more than he should have been able to call up at his age.

Which means there is a mystery at play. There is the question of who gave him the shortcut to power, who had taught him what he needed quickly enough for him to use it, but without teaching him about the downsides or the dangers. Hell, without teaching him about the law. Someone out there put a necromancer into play without prepping him to survive. Someone basically hung this kid out to dry. Maybe it had something to do with that weird tentacle thing I saw coming off the back of his neck. I don't know; there's not really a way for me to find out.

Everyone sees magic differently, so there isn't a book where I can look up 'weird pulsating tentacle thing' to find out. Actually, there probably *is* a book where I could look that up. Dozens of them, even, each with a different explanation. But I don't know if any of them would be the right answer, or at least the right answer I was looking for.

That's the problem with magic. Too many things are true. Too much mythology is right. What religion, folklore, mythos, or whatever has it right? All of them. And none of them. Are vampires bound to the darkness, sparkly, or demons in human form? Yep. And not really. The Maori myths are just as true as the Sioux myths, the Greek myths, or the modern American myths. And just as wrong.

Necromancy is always magic with the dead, but it doesn't always work the same way. Some necromancers, like my old friend Dave, can do it without hurting anyone or anything. Others need to kill to power their magic. Hopefully, the kid didn't have to kill anyone. Not that it matters beyond the fact that someone else would be dead.

The kid's fucked; there's no way around that. Whether he was manipulated or not, he committed a pretty nasty crime. He did it of his own free will. You can't force someone to be a necromancer. He did the crime, and he'd end up doing the time. If he's lucky. If only he hadn't used soul fire on me. If there had been a chance of redemption for him, he probably would've ended up seeing the sun again in a few decades, with far better control over his abilities and a much healthier respect for the law. Not the human law.

Our law.

But in the meantime, there's someone out there who unleashed this kid on the world. And why? Why would he do that? Was it just a matter of damnation, or of binding spirits to the world?

I need to get on this. They haven't assigned me to it yet, but they probably will. This happened on my turf, in my territory. It happened while I was investigating a manifested ghost. So it literally tied into another case; may even be part of the same case. Odds are, I'll get tapped to figure this out. But probably not until the man behind the curtain ruins at least one more human life. And given the chance, I'd prefer to stop him *before* that happens.

Which means I'm going to need to talk to a friend of mine. One with connections. When you're looking for someone damning young men, there's no expert like a Succubus.

So I walk back across the First Street bridge, find my car (the magic doesn't work on me, but it looks like it worked on everyone else—there's nothing broken or missing), and take a ride down Hennepin until it hits Lake. Fully ensconced in uptown, right about where Lyndale and Lake meet, is where my succubus friend will be, even at this time of night.

Maxine DeFleur, as she calls herself, works at a fetish boutique. Maxine has always been kinky, even for her own kind, and I guess she likes being around all the bondage and the leather. Or at least she likes the sexual energy of the store.

When I first met Max, she told me that she was doing her best to stop killing people. Succubi don't have to kill to feed. She can feed just a bit from someone during sex, or she can feed bits and pieces from ambient sexual energy. It's like taking mouthfuls of fog when you really want a glass of water, but it helps keep the edge off. And it helps her avoid killing.

Not that she has a problem with it. She never kept track of how many men and women she's killed, but she did once tell me that she'd done the math, and she was responsible for at least thirty thousand people. Which really sounds like a lot. But over the course of almost eighteen hundred years, it really isn't. Or so she claimed.

Your average succubus needs three to five sexual partners a week. There are fifty-two weeks in a year. On the high end, that's two hundred and sixty a year. Meaning at her age she could easily have passed the half a million mark of sexual encounters. If she killed them all, that would be bad. Instead, she has about double the number of partners, but tries really hard not to kill any of them. She's managed to get down to five percent or less of them dying. Still a pretty nasty amount, but given she has no soul and no conscience, it's pretty fucking impressive.

Of course, she's not being altruistic. She's being a coward. Kill too many people, and a hero starts coming after you. Enough heroes come after you, sooner or later you get killed. And that has always been inconvenient for her. Three times, apparently, was enough.

I come into the shop while Maxine is talking to a young couple about the delicious possibilities of combining a collar that has a strap down the back with additional shackles for the hands with gravity boots to hang upside down and a wartenberg wheel. Her breasts heave just a bit as she talks about it, and she licks her lips as she tastes their arousal. She's all but humping their legs at this point. It would be kind of disgusting if I didn't know how much they were all enjoying it. And if I didn't know Max worked on commission, sort of.

After she rings the couple up for a couple hundred dollars' worth of merchandise, and gives them her phone number, they leave the store. She takes one last deep breath, then smiles at me, her lips positively predatory.

"AJ," she says, caressing my name in a way that makes me feel all the right kinds of dirty. "Are you finally here to shop? I've got lots of goodies I can show you."

I smile. Maxine could make the tax code sound laced with sexual innuendo. "I'm sure you do, Max. But I'm here on business."

Her smile is replaced by a bit of a pout, one that I'm sure has gotten her out of trouble before. "I've been a good girl," she says. Then she smirks. "Well, that's not true. But I've been getting plenty of spankings for my transgressions."

I laugh and shake my head. "Not that kind of business, Max. I actually need your expertise." I hold up a hand to stop her before she can slink towards me. "Not *that* expertise," I say. "The kind about what you did for a living way back in the day."

She looks confused. "Tattoos not paying the bills?" she asks. "You want to be a whore?" A quick shrug. "I'm sure I can help you find the right places. And give you some pointers. We'd have to have some hands-on training, of course, but—"

I shake my head. "No. I mean *way* back in the day. Like back when you only spoke one language."

She lets out a whistle. "You need help with acquisitions? Why on Earth would you get involved in that racket?"

"I'm not. But I think someone else might be, and I need to ask some questions about how it all works."

She looks uncomfortable. I can understand that. It's not every day someone comes to a demon and asks her how a soul might be sold or lost, even just hypothetically. "Okay," she says. "But you gotta understand, I worked in acquisitions, not sales."

"What's the difference?"

She smirks. "I was better at it. The sales people have to offer something in exchange. I just helped people along the path until they were more than willing to just give it up."

I shake my head. I like Maxine, and it's hard to remember that she is a soulless demon, whose sole purpose for existing is to corrupt men (and women) to the service of evil. Or the dark side, or whatever you call it.

"How did you do that?"

She gestures down to her body. "I'd usually just tempt them with a bit of sin here and there. Then I'd let them push the boundaries. Anything you want, I'll let you do it." She gives me a wink. "Oh, you want to try a new position? Absolutely. A new hole? Sure, why not. You want to tie me up?" She holds out her wrists as if to be cuffed. "I'll scream in pleasure if you hurt me. Whipping not good enough anymore? Let's take it up a notch." Then she waves her hands over and over. "And so on and so forth." She shrugs. "Sooner or later, they're doing things they never thought they would, and it's no big deal. Only it was their choice. Every step of the way."

"You really are a snake," I say.

"Honey, I've got a lot more to offer than a fucking apple."

An image comes to mind, one that I'm going to have to scrub out at some point. Or maybe recall next time I'm having trouble getting off during sex. Either way, can't keep focusing on it right now. "Okay, okay, I get the point," I say. "But what about sales? How does *that* usually work?"

She shrugs. "Your guess is more or less as good as mine. Someone contacts a demon, offers to sell their soul, negotiations start, and then a contract gets signed."

"Always a written contract?"

"Nah." She shakes her head. "Sometimes it's verbal. Sealed with a kiss. Or a handshake. Or anything, really. So long as the sap knows what he's doing."

"And what can you get for a soul?"

She gives me a stern look. "Ashley Jasmine Abigaile Grey," she says, "you'd better not be in the market."

"First of all, that's not my name." She shrugs, not caring. "Second of all, Jasmine is a way better middle name than mine." She nods at that one. "And third of all, I'm not looking to sell. I'm trying to figure out how a high school kid managed to get the mojo to bind a spirit and then drain it to power soul fire."

She lets out a whistle. "That's some pretty serious shit," she says. "I don't really know much about magic. Never learned it myself—too much math. But necromancy isn't a high school kind of thing. That's something old people do."

"So he'd need to sell his soul?"

She shrugs. "He could have been some kind of genius savant."

"He wasn't."

"Trained since birth by the all-time father-of-the-year winner?"

I shake my head.

"Then yeah, he probably sold his soul."

"To who?"

She shrugs. "I'm no accountant," she says. "They keep track of that shit. He could have sold it to anyone with horns." She taps her head, her hair laying on perfect skin, completely lacking in the huge fuck-off horns I know she *can* grow. "And it wasn't me."

"Because you don't do that shit anymore," I say, only the smallest edge of menace in my voice.

"I *never* did that shit," she says. "Too much like work. I was fine just seeing what I could get people to do on their own. Tempting people and playing harsher and harsher scenes is *fun*. But I don't do that anymore. And I haven't done that in over a thousand years." She takes a breath. "Now. What do you say we go dancing? I'm hungry."

"Don't you have to work?"

She shrugs. "I can close if I want to. It's my shop." And it's not like she needs the money. Maxine is terrible with money. Her businesses fail constantly. But ever since interest was invented, she's been putting money aside. Usually, she forgets about it for a while. Then, when she finds an old bank account, voila! Instant money. Being a prostitute for a few hundred years when she didn't need to buy food and never got sick or pregnant probably helped too. As did her never really needing a pimp. Though I imagine the pimps that did try to control her, at the start, ended up with her acquisitions accounts. It's not easy for a demon to really retire.

"I'm working. I need to figure out who bought this kid's soul."

"So we'll go to Ground Zero. It's one of their goth nights. If it's a high school kid, odds are that's where he met the demon anyway."

She slinks towards me, a pleading look on her face, pouting in her lips, and mischief in her eyes. "Please, AJ? It's so hard to find someone to go out with who I don't want to sleep with."

Most girls would've talked about someone who doesn't want to sleep with them. But I know better. Everyone wants to sleep with Max. Everyone. It's not even a conscious thing. Spend enough time around her, breathe in those pheromones, and you're going to want her. Or at least, have some naughty thoughts about her. Some people are smart and learn to keep their distance.

I roll my eyes. "Most people would be offended by that," I tell her.

She shrugs. "Most people would think it was because I didn't find them attractive."

"So you do think I'm attractive?"

She laughs, and refuses to even dignify a response. "You're just not my type. You know that."

Maxine is a Succubus. A sex demon. Anything with a pulse should, in theory, be her type. I mean, I've heard of the occasional Succubus having to come out and admit that they were heterosexual—it usually doesn't go well, and they tend to get pretty shunned in the community. But Max isn't heterosexual. Not by a long shot. She is, however, submissive. Entirely. As she would say, the only time there's a dominant bone in her body is while she's getting fucked.

So I'm not her type. And she's not mine. Doesn't mean we can't be friends. And doesn't mean I can't keep an eye on her to make sure she doesn't start killing people left and right.

"Fine," I say. "We can go to Zero."

"Fantastic!" she says, clapping her hands like a giddy school girl. Then she looks me up and down. "You're not going to wear that, are you?"

INTERLUDE THREE

She starts when the gavel slams down. She doesn't say anything when his mother calls her a murderer. She doesn't say anything to the reporters outside. She doesn't speak when the microphones are shoved into her face, or when the flashing cameras blind her.

She doesn't speak at all until they try to remove her bracelet. She begs them not to. She doesn't want the magic. She doesn't want to go back to normal. She just wants to die like her boyfriend.

She spends three days in a hospital, locked in a room all by herself. They take the bracelet. She burns the padding off the walls, her hair once more burned away. They give her the bracelet back.

She doesn't speak again for weeks. It's not until someone comes over, a friend of the family, and tells her he can bind her magic for her, permanently, that she says anything, that she finally makes eye contact with another human being.

"It's going to hurt," he tells her. "More than anything has ever hurt you before."

She scoffs. "Nothing can hurt me more," she says.

He ties her down anyway. Holds her head down, chin to chest.

He draws on the back of her neck, and that feels good. But then the needle starts.

She screams. She screams a lot. It hurts so much, like someone peeling off her skin. She begs him to stop, but he just keeps going. She pulls at the rope, but there is no give. He knew what he was doing. He whispers to her, being as reassuring as he can be, telling her to hold out just a little bit longer. It's almost over. Just a little bit more. It'll be okay.

And then the pain stops, gone just as suddenly as it had started. The area on the back of her neck burns, but the burning doesn't bother her. And when he takes the bracelet off, she gasps, expecting to erupt in flames again.

But there are no flames. Just a general warmth.

She thanks him with her eyes, glad that he tortured her, because the torture fixed her.

As he unties her, and her parents come to check that she is okay, she looks at him with awe in her eyes. "How did you do that?"

He smiles at her. "It's magic," he says. "Same principle as the bracelet, but more focused and more permanent."

She has hated magic so much, she never thought it could do anything good. "Can you bind magic for anyone?"

"I can do a lot," he tells her. "These tattoos are all powered by my magic." He shows her his arms, sleeves of mystical runes wrapping up both arms. "It hurts, though."

"It wasn't so bad," she lies.

He laughs. "Of course not," he says. "Even still, I won't get one unless I'm ready for it."

"How do you know when you're ready?"

He shrugs. "It comes with understanding the magic," he says. "You can't hide from it. If you do, it's just going to make itself known. Suddenly, violently, and all over the place." He gives her a sad smile, because he knows it already has.

She thanks him. She cries, but the tears are different. The movie finally has a happy ending.

CHAPTER FOUR

After a few minutes of argument, a few minutes of picking things out, and about an hour of wriggling into another outfit, Maxine is finally willing to let me leave the store. She convinces me to at least let her polish my boots (though I tell her she has to use actual polish, and that I won't wear them while she does it, which she finds disappointing), and then gets me into leather pants that are so tight I shouldn't be able to bend my knees in them. But they're very well designed, and while the black leather lays so flush to my skin that touching it is like touching my bare leg, I can move pretty easily. I can even do a high kick, if necessary. Or kneel, as the pants are intended to allow.

I'm not fond of the corset she put me in though. It leaves my arms bare, which is good, but the steel boning in the corset make it impossible to bend too much and difficult to breathe in. Not something I'd want to wear in a fight. Though the corset *would* probably stop a knife. She pulls it so tight I feel like she's dug the ribbon into my back, then yanks it a bit tighter. Then she convinces me to add a simple leather collar and wrist shackles to complete the look. Well, I end up with a wrist shackle on my left wrist. The one on my right won't stay closed, thanks to a skeleton key I have inked to my wrist. But it still looks good. And it's not like I'm going to let someone tie me up.

The price tag mounts up pretty fast. If I were to buy the outfit, I'd be coming awfully close to four digits. But Max doesn't even ask. She just cuts off the price tags and goes to get herself ready. Like I said, she's terrible with money.

When she comes down, my sexuality comes into question. I may generally prefer boys, but I've been known to play around. But for just a few seconds, all thoughts of men rush out of my head, and I only have eyes for her.

Her boots are black leather, laced up front from the top of her foot all the way up above her knees. There's no zipper, either; these are the real deal. The two inches of platform and the five inches of heel make her about as tall as I am. The metalwork on the heel draws the eye and makes you think naughty things, which is of course the point.

From the top of the boots there is some creamy white skin visible, more than enough to get the mind going, only to disappear into what looks like the flimsiest skirt in the history of the universe. It's multiple pieces, all of them able to move, so that with every step, you have to wonder if she's about to flash you. Like it's only a matter of time before you see her underwear.

Maxine can read surface thoughts, especially when they are sexual in nature and about her. "I don't believe in underwear," she says, literally reading my mind. "It gets in the way and serves no real purpose. Like Canada."

Her torso is in a corset so tight it makes mine look like a loose hanging t-shirt. I'm pretty sure I could get my fingers to touch around her waist. A human woman would probably be dead, or at least need a lot of very slow and careful training to get that small. I think Dita Von Teese can do it, but even she doesn't hold a candle to Max. Though to be fair, Max does insist that Dita is a very attentive student.

Her arms disappear into black leather gloves at about the

elbow, the laces over a strip of purple along the back of her arm, sending the tiny jolt of color out all the way down to the back of her palm, just before her fingers slide out of the gloves, coming to long and stunningly gorgeous purple nails that every salon wishes they could provide.

She's got a collar on, with a little pendant hanging from it, but I'm positive it's only there to show off her breasts. It's not fair comparing breasts with Max. She's a demon. She's literally built to be sexy. That said, her chest isn't all that big. She's got a nice medium sized set, very pretty but not overwhelming. It fits her perfectly. Like mine do after all that exercise.

Her red hair is tied in two loose braids, forming little pigtails tied with black satin ribbon. She calls them handholds (though not as effective as her horns, she insists), and their innocence makes her look that much more decadent.

So with all that, it's no real surprise that the eyes follow her when we get to the club. I don't think even the people standing outside in the cold, waiting to be let in, begrudge her walking right up to the front and inside without so much as pretending to pay the cover charge. There are some eyes on me, but it's like I'm the consolation prize. Which is fine, because fuck those guys. I'm not here to be a sex object. In fact, I wouldn't be wearing this ridiculous outfit at all if it weren't for Maxine. I don't even have anywhere to hide my knives.

What I do have is a lot of exposed skin. Enough to show the ankh tattoo on my collarbone and the top of the claw slash across my chest. On my back are the tips of my wings. Which, unlike Maxine's, aren't real. That tattoo just helps me survive a fall. Hers actually sprout and let her fly. You can see the thick black arrows on each of my shoulders, covering up glyphs that it's better for human eyes not to see. My hands, with the two tats on each finger, are visible. And so is the key on my wrist. And then there are a few little ones to finish off the sleeve on my left arm, the symbol on the back of my neck, the one behind my ear, and a little hint of the one at the bottom of my back, should I ever be able to actually bend over enough to show it.

All of my tattoos mean something. But some of them mean a lot. And not just in the sense that they have a personal meaning. They *do* something. Every single one of them is a spell carved into my flesh. Each one represents hours of torture binding magic into myself. And then usually several more hours to cover them up and hide the magic so I don't drive people crazy when they check me out.

Max has some ink too. But her ink isn't even real. Or rather, it is. It's not tattoos. It's just pictographic representations of the limited shapeshifting she can pull off. So it's where her wings, her tail, and her horns hide. She doesn't have one for her claws; I don't know why. Maybe it's hidden under her fingernails. Whatever it is, she didn't sit for even a minute to get those done. Bitch just had them when she got her body.

She didn't choose Ground Zero at random. She didn't choose it because it's so close to University. And she didn't choose it because she's a regular. She had another reason. Ulterior motives are the best kind, especially when dealing with hell spawn. If she's bringing me here, right after I asked about selling and buying souls, it's because someone in here can do it. And it's probably not a coincidence that Riverview is like five blocks from here. If the kid sold his soul, this is probably where he did it. Which means someone in here needs a good talking to. Possibly the kind of talking to that leaves concussions and contusions.

Of course, finding him in this crowd isn't going to be a cakewalk. My butt is tingling like mad. There's an eye of Horus on my left cheek and an eye of Ra on the other. Well, not exactly on the cheek, but low enough to not really count as my back either. And I didn't get them just so people would think I was looking back when they stare at my ass, or to freak people out during sex if we choose the right position—that's just a perk. The tats are there because that's the base of my spine, the core of my being. Which means it's the best place to get the feelings. And those two eyes give me feelings. Tingly feelings. Any time I get close to anything supernatural, the ink starts to tingle.

Everything has its own vibe too. A vampire just makes the eye of Horus tingle, mostly around the pupil. Werewolves make the whole eye of Ra feel like it's shivering. Ghosts make Horus feel cold. Witches tend to make the eye of Ra itch really badly. Except necromancers. Most dead things, or creatures that deal with dead things, I can feel in the eye of Horus. Most live things in the eye of Ra. It's not exactly a good or bad guy detector. But it's better than nothing.

Maxine doesn't make either one tingle, by the way. She makes me tingle somewhere else, somewhere I don't want to talk about in mixed company. Or any company, really. And her tingling isn't because of tattoos.

"Don't worry," she says, once again picking up my thoughts. "I can't eat you. You'd be perfectly safe with me. If anything, I'd be the one who has to worry."

"What do you mean?"

"All that," she says, gesturing to my body kind of generally. "Your energy is all bound up. I can't get at it. So I can't feed from you. No matter how turned on you get, you're like a void to me."

"Then why do you tease me so much?"

She shrugs and gives me a smirk. "It's fun," she says. Then she takes me by the hand and leads me onto the dance floor.

I'm not a succubus, but even I can smell the arousal on the floor. Dancing can be so sexual, and there's so much floating in the air. Within a few seconds, I start to feel a bit lightheaded. That's Max's influence. She just exudes pheromones and endorphins, whether she wants to or not. Makes people relax. Makes them do things they might not otherwise do. Who ever said demons had to play fair?

Somehow, knowing where it's coming from makes it both

easier to resist and easier to let go. If I know I need to resist, I can. But I don't; I can trust Max. I mean, as much as you can ever trust a demon. I know Maxine is scared of me. She doesn't want me to kill her (she keeps telling me that being killed three times was enough for her; I don't really know what she means by that), and she knows that I will blame her if anything bad happens to me while under her influence. So it's trust based on fear. Which is sometimes the best kind.

But since I can trust her, I let myself go and let the music pump through me. There's a lot out there that I can't feel anymore. I can't feel the heat in a sauna, I can't feel the cut of a winter breeze. But I can still feel bass pumping through my body. I can still feel the music reach out and take control of my body, feel it thrum through my bones.

I toss my head to the beat, and as I do, the hair comes away from my septagram. I can see the energy in the club. The first time I saw Max like this, it scared the shit out of me. Everyone has an aura. Max doesn't. When there's sexual energy in the air, all the other auras in the room start to lean towards her, little wisps of them getting sucked into her body like she's some kind of black hole. Mine doesn't go to her, I'm told. I don't know; you can't see your own aura. But mine is apparently so under lock and key that it doesn't go to her.

But everyone else does. And I know when she stops, the auras will go back to normal. Nothing will seem amiss. But everyone's aura will be ever so slightly smaller than it was when she came in. It's not exactly dangerous, and the bit that's missing heals usually overnight, but the fact of the matter is that Maxine DeFleur is, quite literally, sipping people's souls.

She could just pick one target and probably suck them dry. But she doesn't do that. She does this little light tasting thing, because it lets her get her fix, lets her stay fed, without anyone being seriously hurt. It's like if instead of having to kill off one of your sheep, you flicked each one on the ear. Annoying, maybe, but not worth getting upset about.

I just compared people to sheep, didn't I? Fuck, I've been doing this too long.

I use the opportunity to look around the rest of the club. That tightly wound energy that seems to pulse without ever actually moving—that's a vampire. The aura that's so bright it starts to push on the auras of those around it—that's a werewolf. Those three faded auras—those are ghosts.

And that one over there, in the back of the club, the guy who has no aura at all—that's a demon.

I pull myself free of Maxine's influence, and of the thrumming of the beat on the dance floor, and make a beeline towards that demon. Max might be kinda flighty, but she does things for a reason. It's the right kind of club for that wannabe kid to hang out in. The music is right. Michelle, my little silent partner ghost, is still out on the floor dancing. She looks comfortable here. Probably been here before, which makes it that much more likely that Ground Zero is more than a clever name in this particular case.

Michelle is not scared of the demon, but she's not getting any closer to him either.

He sees me coming and makes some kind of gesture that makes his cronies vamoose. I cover up my septagram so I can actually look at him without being distracted by all the things around us. He might try to do something to me, but I'm guessing he knows better than that.

He gestures to an open seat, and I sit down with my back to the dance floor. I hate having my back to the room, and there's only so far I can really trust Max to watch my back. Still, I wanted this meeting, so suck it up, AJ.

"To what do I owe the dubious pleasure?" he asks.

"I'm looking for a salesman, or at least an accountant."

He smiles. "I don't think I know what you're talking about. I'm in the entertainment industry."

I frown. I hate it when they play games. "My name is Ashley Grey," I say. "Maybe you've heard of me."

His smile gets somehow wider and even more smarmy. "I have heard of you, Miss Grey. Can I take the fact that you are sitting here talking to me as you intending to settle things peacefully?"

No one ever remembers all the times you talked things down. They just remember the explosions and the body counts. I'm never going to live that one down. It was one time. *One.* "I'm just here for information," I say. "As far as I can tell, you haven't done anything explicitly wrong. I'm just trying to get some details."

"Details are expensive, Miss Grey."

My fingers twitch. Even my hands want to just throttle this guy.

"A kid sold his soul to get the necromantic power to bind his dead crush's spirit so he could have a girlfriend in the creepiest way possible. I need to know the terms of the deal."

"That is a hefty request. And what are you offering in return?"

"Well, I'm guessing the contract is about to be expedited. Doesn't that count for anything?"

The demon shakes his head and picks up a glass with some kind of amber liquid in it. I'm going to guess whiskey, because I have no real idea. I'm not a drinker; the only reason I know about Melon Balls is because of my friend (who is a drinker) who introduced me to them and then made me memorize what was in them. It could be some kind of amber liquor. But it's probably whiskey. Or scotch. Is scotch that color? I don't know.

He swirls the liquid around a bit and then raises the glass to his lips and takes a drink. I think that makes it brandy. "What you've already done is already done," he says. "That isn't payment. It's coincidence. Try again."

"I could not expose the fact that you're wheeling and dealing with forbidden magics."

"Dealing isn't forbidden."

"That kind of necromancy is."

He shrugs. "We are not responsible for the outcomes of any deals. Once contracts are signed, all liability is taken up by the signer, and any rights to dispute or slander the deal maker are forfeit."

Fucking demons. "Look, are you going to tell me what I want to know?"

"I may. I'm certainly willing. But everything has its price."

"And what do you want?"

"A favor."

I shake my head. "No. Absolutely not. You think I'm new? I'm not going to agree to just owe you a favor. Are you high?"

He chuckles. "Fair enough, fair enough." He puts the glass down and taps a finger on the table. It sounds like expensive crystal clinking together after a toast. "How would you feel about trading a spell for the information? A skin spell, specifically."

I take a deep breath and lean back. "Those are expensive," I say. "Especially if you want something intricate. How about this: I'll give you one hour of tattoo work for every three questions you answer honestly."

He smiles. Demons love these games. "They have to be yes or no questions," he says. I nod. "Deal." He reaches a hand across the table.

I shake it, which is not something I like to do. Deals with demons can be sealed a lot of ways. Sometimes it's signing a contract, sometimes it's exchanging a kiss, sometimes it's just a hand shake. Doesn't matter which—it's all personal style on the demon's part. But every one of them is just as binding. "Ask your questions."

"Did you recently purchase a teenager's soul in exchange for necromantic power?" I'm glad I added the recently. I have no idea how old this demon is. He'd be telling the truth even if it had happened a thousand years ago.

"No."

Well, shit. That puts a damper on things.

"Do you know who did?"

"Yes."

He's smiling. I hate it when they smile. He has that look on his face like he thinks he's so much more clever than me. Like there's something I'm not catching. Something that lets him get away with whatever nasty work he did.

Okay. Try again. "Do you know who I arrested earlier?"

He frowns. "Yes."

Ha ha, bitch. Take that.

"Did you purchase his soul?"

"Yes." That one comes out as little more than a growl.

"Is that the only soul you've purchased in the last month?"

He smiles. "No."

One more question, and then he gets two hours. Any longer than that and he might ask for something nasty. Two hours is already kind of pushing it. One more.

Inspiration strikes. "Does this have to do with why Michelle is sticking around?"

"Yes."

Okay. So that's helpful. I'm not sure how helpful, or what it means, but it's better than I had a minute ago.

"Deal's up," I say. "I owe you two hours of tattoo work."

"Of magical tattoo work."

I nod.

"And that's time spent tattooing. Drawing and planning you do on your own. That was the deal."

I did agree to give him two hours of tattooing, not two hours of my time. Fuck. I nod again. "You can't hold on to this and exchange it for something at a later date," I remind him. "It was two hours of tattoo work, not two hours of my time or of my life."

He nods. "I have no intention to transfer those hours. I will collect on them soon."

Soon is a relative term. "You better do it before I get arthritis. Two hours won't go nearly as far if I have an injury or just slow down."

I tap the table and stand up. "It's been... well, it happened."

"Until next time, Miss Grey."

I wanted to throw him some kind of quip, some insistence that there wouldn't be a next time. But I agreed to two hours. So there will *definitely* be a next time. And if I said there wouldn't, I might technically be violating the deal, reneging on my side of the payment. And you don't want to renege on a deal with a demon. I don't know how their laws work, but I know that things would be settled with his laws, not mine.

Which means not in my favor.

INTERLUDE FOUR

That was my first tattoo. I was fifteen. I had murdered my boyfriend with my magic, and I didn't want anything to do with it. But I did want to understand it. I wanted to know how it worked, so I knew how to bind it in the future. I didn't want to hide from it; I wanted to hunt it down.

I didn't go back to school. There were only a few weeks left in the year anyway. I'd have to retake my sophomore year, but I didn't care. I didn't want to go back there anyway. I couldn't go back there. Not to that school. Not to those people.

I spent the summer learning about magic. How to see it, how to track it. I learned about how to bind it, too. The family friend, Jason, lent me a book about binding magic. I tore through it in a weekend, then started following the bibliography, reading everything that book cited. My parents let me buy a bunch of books from various vendors, and I soon had a pretty decent sized library. By the end of the summer, Jason was borrowing a book from me.

I went back to school in the fall. Well, I went *to* school. A new school, an hour away from the old school. On the other side of the city. I was a completely new face, a sophomore who could drive, and I had a tattoo. I thought for sure I'd get to be cool.

I heard the first rumors about me during lunch that first day. Was I that girl that murdered her boyfriend? Wasn't I a pyromaniac?

I thought I'd get over it. I turned inward. I read books at lunch. I tried not to care, not to notice the whispers.

Then, in a chemistry class, kids were seeing how long they could hold their hands over their bunsen burner. I was still "new kid," and they dared me to try. No way I could hold my hand longer than they could. I was afraid of fire, right?

So I held my hand over the flame. And I held it. Eventually, I got distracted and looked away, not paying attention to my hand.

Then someone screamed. I looked at my hand, and it was *in* the flame. But I didn't feel it. It didn't hurt.

The teacher came over and yanked my hand out of the flame, yelling at me for being so stupid. He ended up yelling at the whole class for being careless, and sent me to the nurse despite my insistence that it didn't hurt.

She gave me detention for ditching class and for lying to her about why.

I never went back to that school.

CHAPTER FIVE

Talking to demons left a bad taste in my mouth. One that I can only get rid of with a cigarette. And I really don't feel like dancing anymore. So I step outside and light up, wishing that I didn't need my lighter. I'm a witch, and my primary element is fire. But I can't summon up enough of a flame to light a cigarette. It's kind of pathetic.

Of course, I can also walk through an inferno without even breaking a sweat, so long as I avoid the smoke inhalation. So it's a tradeoff.

Maxine comes out when I move on to my second cancer stick. I probably shouldn't call them that; that's what my sister calls them whenever she's trying to get me to quit. I think I adopted the name out of spite. Maxine is panting, which makes her breasts heave, which I'm sure is not an accident. There's a big old smile on her face, and her skin is almost glowing. She grabs one of my cigarettes and leans forward, bending so her butt sticks out just right and pressing the one between her lips against mine, lighting her smoke from my cherry.

So many dirty jokes, so little time.

"So did that help?" she asks.

"Yes and no," I say. "I got a hint, but it didn't really help all that much. Wasn't really worth the price."

"What did you give him?"

"Two hours of ink."

She nods. "At least you'll get to hurt him."

That does make me laugh. Maxine is good at that. I take a long drag from my cancer stick (because fuck you, Darien, that's why), feeling the smoke in my lungs, the only way I can really feel heat. It's nice, it's comforting. I hate it when I lose my core heat. It doesn't happen often, but smoking helps. A lot.

"Look, Max, about the clothes—"

She holds up a hand. "Keep them," she says. "Just make sure to tell people where you got them, and come dancing with me again sometime soon."

"Okay." I look down at my watch as if I don't know how late it's getting. "I have got to go to bed," I say.

She raises an eyebrow and smirks. "Is that an invitation?"

"No," I say, smiling back at her. "Just a statement. You need a ride anywhere?"

She glances back at the club. "I think I can find a ride just fine."

"No killing anyone."

She holds up her hand in a boy scout salute. "I solemnly swear I am up to no good." She winks. "I mean, I promise not to kill anyone who doesn't try to kill me first."

Like Max could do much of anything in a fight. I've seen her try. It's actually pretty adorable, and only a little bit pathetic. But it's a promise of sorts, and it's the best I'm going to get from her. She gives me a smirk, a wink, and a toss of her hips as she walks back into the club, flicking away her cigarette, not even half finished, before heading back inside.

I turn the other way and take off towards home. It's been a long day, and I've got a half decent bed that's just calling my name.

INTERLUDE FIVE

y parents called their friend to find out what was going on; Jason and I talked about what happened, and he helped me understand two very important things about magic. Magic doesn't come from nowhere. And, more importantly, there are always prices to be paid. My hand in the flame was just the beginning of the first tattoo. I was immune to fire, but with that came an inability to feel the heat. I didn't even feel warm with my hand in the flames. And I didn't feel any heat in the shower. I was seventeen, and the rest of my life was going to be spent taking cold showers.

He did tell me that it wasn't entirely permanent. As my magic grew, I'd begin to feel something, at least. But I would never feel heat the way most people do. My nerves, essentially, were dead to temperature. Which also meant I didn't really get cold, an important point for Chicago.

It was late September. The nearest school I could find was too far away. My parents let me home school.

My little sister started high school that year. She didn't have any trouble, beyond a few people asking about her crazy pyromaniac sister. She got in a few fights, nothing serious. People stopped picking on her to her face, warning each other that she might curse them if they said anything to her face.

She was home schooled the next year. Which was good; when her magic started to develop, we knew what to look for. We knew how to get her help.

And I realized it was time for another tattoo.

I called Jason on my own. Asked him if he would come bind more magic into me. He didn't want to. I was still too young. Seventeen is still too young to get a tattoo, let alone a second one. I told him I would do it myself if he didn't help me.

He scoffed, and then I told him I'd been studying tattoo methods, and had learned about the slow poking method. I told him I knew I had to use silver needles.

He started taking me more seriously. Told me to hold out until I finished the school year, then he would ask my parents if I could spend some time with him.

I finished high school two months later, getting my GED a year ahead of schedule. Then I more or less moved in with Jason Anders, leaving my native Chicago and going to the City of Brotherly Garbage. I mean love. Philadelphia is about love. Right.

CHAPTER SIX

I wake up the next day at the ungodly hour of eight o'clock in the morning. I don't know how people do this every day. I'm not waking up of my own free will. I'm only getting up because I have to, because I have to go into the Office.

I know, it's weird to think about going into the office as a tattoo artist. I don't go to that job until about noon. But that's like my day job. My cover career. I also work to keep our laws, which makes me sort of like a cop, only not really. None of the restrictions. The supernatural world doesn't tend to be quite as forgiving as the human world. There's not exactly due process.

Some people have called me a bounty hunter. It's not entirely wrong.

And today, I'm getting assigned to a case. Probably Michelle's, so I'll at least be a leg up. I got the collar on that necromancer kid, so that's something in my favor. Whatever the details are, I have to go in to get them. I hate going in.

Never mind that I have to get up at this unfair hour. Never mind that I need three alarms to wake me up. Never mind that I have to down half a pot of coffee before my brain starts working enough to remember that I need to put shoes on *before* I leave the apartment.

I let a cigarette dangle from my mouth as I open my car and make a quick gamble with the car gods. My 'check engine' light has been on for so long that I think the bulb burned out. It's the only explanation I can think of; I know I didn't fix the fucking thing. The engine turnover thing complains a bit, making me hold the key to the starting point thing as it makes the grinding noise. But it does turn on. Or start up. Or whatever.

I don't know cars. I do tattoos, I do krav maga, and I do magic. I don't do cars.

It starts, and when I press the gas pedal, it goes faster. The brake makes it go slower. The wheel turns it. That's about all I care about. When it gets cold, I care that there's a heater. Actually, that part only really matters if I have passengers. I can't really feel temperature all that much anymore. And, living in Minnesota, I don't miss it. We have temperature deficits here; that's when the weather is so cold that the mercury in a thermometer throws up its hands and says 'nope!'

To most people, Foshay Tower is an old building that became a hotel about a decade back. It used to be the tallest building in the city, but those days are *long* gone. Now it's still visible on the skyline, and you can read the word "Foshay" right on it, but it's only about thirty stories high. Which, if you ask me, is plenty high enough.

What people don't know about Foshay is that there's a thirteenth floor. Back in the day, or whenever Foshay was built, they were still going from twelve straight to fourteen. But when it was renovated in 2006, they inserted an actual thirteenth floor. I don't mean they renumbered the floors. I mean they put one in. One that isn't supposed to be there. One that isn't on the plans, and one that most people still don't know about.

That's where the Office is. If you're supposed to be able to get there, and you know how, you can find it just by taking the elevator. You press the panel where a thirteen *should* be, a little circle lights up to let you know you've done it, and then it opens up on a floor that doesn't technically exist.

That's magic for you.

I tend to get a lot of looks when I go into the tower. Maybe it's because I go in relatively frequently, but I never check in to a room or even ask where someone is staying. I just head right to the elevator without talking to anyone. Maybe it's all the tattoos all over my body. I don't know.

They can't even see most of them today. I'm wearing long sleeves, I'm wearing jeans, and I have my hair braided behind my head. And I have my hands in my pockets. So there's maybe a trace of three or four bits of ink, if they don't look too closely.

Maybe I'm just being paranoid.

It doesn't get much better when I get off the elevator on floor thirteen. There I'm stared at for a whole different reason. I stand out, again, but not from the ink. No, I stand out because I am, or I look, human.

Depending on the time of day, you can run into vampires, werewolves, pixies (nosy fuckers), demons, cherubim, kappa, kitsune, golems, rakshasa—basically anything and everything. They come here to work, to get licenses and visas, to register complaints, or sometimes to face charges. And while some of them look human some of the time, none of them look as human as I do.

So I get stared at.

Thankfully, I've been coming often enough that they don't stare at me like I'm a food delivery anymore. And there are one or two of them that I actually know now.

Like Chuck, who is even now walking towards me. His walk is a little bit of a waddle, to be honest. Gremlins aren't really that long-legged. If he wanted to move faster, he'd use his arms, which are about twice as long. But there's no need to look like a monkey when you're at work. It's not good for the image. Plus, I think he gets paid hourly.

"AJ," he says, his voice like walking on fresh gravel. "I heard a rumor you might be coming in."

I smile at him. We don't shake hands or anything. Gremlins only shake hands when they're making deals. Part of that has to do with those claws that I can't really even see. I know they're there, sharper than diamond, sharp enough to pierce my skin and get a little blood. Not that I'd really notice; the enzymes on his skin would heal the cut almost as fast as I got it. But not so fast as to prevent him from getting blood, and therefore giving him something to use when enforcing a deal.

So yeah, I try not to touch Chuck any more than I have to. I also try not to think about how it must feel for him when he touches himself.

"Last night, some kid tried to bind a girl's soul against her will."

He raises what I like to assume is an eyebrow. Hard to be sure. "Kid? Where'd he get the ability to do that?"

I let out a sigh. "Sold his soul."

Chuck shakes his head. He's not feeling sorry for the kid. He's thinking that the kid is stupid. And he is. "Want some coffee?"

"I'd murder for some," I say.

"Please don't."

He waddles over to the coffee station and brings me back a cup of hot blackness, so dark light can't escape it. It tastes wonderful. Which is weird; I usually don't take my coffee black. But here in the Office, it's a different story.

"So I'm expected then?"

"Only by the rumor mill," he says. "You're still going to have to go to the waiting room. Sorry." He shrugs, and does look apologetic. Chuck's a nice guy. For a gremlin, I mean.

I take my coffee into the waiting room. It's like one of those rooms from the movies, like a dentist's office. Or like hell. Or, worse, the DMV. There are about fifty chairs, all of varying levels of discomfort, and a good half of them are already full, even this early in the morning. Some of them are clutching numbers and staring up at a screen like they're willing their numbers to show up. I don't take a number.

They asked me to be here. I'll wait for a little while, but if no one comes to get me, I'm fucking out of here.

I wish I could smoke. The laws of the human world don't really apply here, but they still don't like people smoking. I think it has to do with prolonging misery. I mean, yeah, smoking can bother non-smokers, but not so much as you'd notice. But not being able to smoke when you really, *really* want one... that's torture. Which I'm convinced in an old language was called "bureaucracy."

The people, or rather the things, clutching numbers seem to have gone all out in trying to look pathetic. Like somehow, sympathy will win them their case, their freedom, or whatever else they came here to get. You never see someone dressed to the nines waiting in a place like this. They're in threadbare sweats, or shirts with all kinds of stains, so many you can't even imagine what the original color was. Some of them look emaciated, like they've been slowly starving to death as they wait.

That's all bullshit. No one waits more than two hours. It's policy. But people sometimes try to look like they've been there for days. Maybe it's just the way they look, or maybe they're trying to get special treatment.

I say that like I'm not going to get special treatment. I didn't pick a number. I don't have to. I'm special, and someone—probably Stewart, my handler—is going to come and get me.

In the meantime, I have to sit here and try not to get looked at. For a lot of these people, I'm the reason they're here. I, or someone like me, caught them doing something they shouldn't, or they just want to avoid having to deal with someone like me. I've got a bit of a reputation—some of it earned, most of it not—and I'd rather not have to deal with an angry imp or some shit like that.

But there really isn't much to do. There are magazines, but I'm pretty sure they carefully select them in such a way that they will be of absolutely zero interest to anyone. I think that every time someone picks up a magazine, they take it away and replace it. Which gives only a few recent magazines, and a shitload of things that practically predate the printing press. Not the good kind of old things either. If there was something in here about a treatise on ancient magicks, I'd be all over that shit. But it's more like talking about the scandal of someone showing off her ankle at the beach.

God, I need a cigarette.

Two people get called in before Stewart shows up. One of them looks vaguely human, certainly able to pass, and the other is, I think, a goblin. Short, squat, mean looking, but all smiles, moving and chattering like a grandma. Seems about right.

When Stewart does finally bring me back, he at least has the courtesy to offer me a smoke, even lighting it with an old fashioned wood match. They say that makes things taste better, but I guess I'm just a philistine; to me it tastes like nicotine. Wonderful nicotine. And it takes the edge off, making me that much less likely to kill people who look at me funny.

"Coffee?" he asks.

I've finished the cup that Chuck gave me. And you can never have too much of it, I guess. I'm about to agree, when he offers me an energy drink instead.

Even better.

We go to his office, which might qualify as a broom closet if it were a little bigger, and we somehow manage to both fit inside. He sucks in his almost nonexistent gut to slide around his desk, and I close the door so that I can sit in the chair across from it.

"What's the word on the kid?" I ask.

"He is in a holding cell. Trial is tomorrow. Execution probably following immediately."

I shake my head. "That's a shame. He sold his soul for that power."

Stewart looks at me and puts his hands together, intertwining his fingers on the desk. He lets out a long sigh. "He did," not quite a question, not quite a statement. "Signed it away just for the power?"

I nod. "He wanted to bind a girl he liked, make her his girlfriend. Stupid teenager bullshit."

"You think he can be rehabilitated? Learn to control his magic, learn to use it properly?"

That's why I like Stewart. He's always trying to save people, even from the trouble they get themselves into.

I shrug. I don't want to commit to anything. Kid sold his soul, and that's on him. He was the one dumb enough to do it. If he made that stupid of a decision once, he might make a worse one in the future.

Having sold his soul, there are really only two options for him: accept the loss and go to hell when he dies, or find something that the demon wants more than his soul. And whatever that something is, it's almost certainly going to be much, much worse than what he's done so far.

"Anything's possible," I say. "But I wouldn't put it past him to find alternate payments. Maybe bind some of the dead for the demon. Or do something worse. If we don't convict him now, he's just going to do something much worse later."

"But do we need to execute him?"

"Those are your laws," I say. "I just work here. If you think you can hold him in a cell, then go right ahead. No skin off my back. But sooner or later, that kid's gonna burn."

"You do not seem that terribly bothered by it." He frowns, almost as if he's disappointed in me.

"Why the fuck should I?" I ask. "This kid was dumb enough to sell his *soul*, then tried to bind the soul of a girl who recently died, one who probably didn't even know he existed, so he could live out some perverted fantasy about her falling in love with him. And she would have; he would have forced her to, basically raping her, over and over again. So no, I've got no pity for him. He's reckless, he's an idiot, and he made a huge fucking mistake."

"But that is just it!" he says. "He made a mistake. One little error."

I laugh. "It wasn't a *little* error. Selling your soul isn't a *little* error. And don't forget that he bound Michelle, and now she can't move on."

"Michelle is the girl?"

I nod.

"And you are going to help her move on?"

"If I can. I'm not really sure how. I can't hear her, I can just see her. So until a series of yes and no questions bears fruit, I really have no idea."

"You should get a Ouija board."

"Fuck Parker Brothers."

Stewart smiles. He does that a lot. It's gentle, it's almost—but not quite—condescending, and it's a little bit infectious. But he doesn't press the point. Just moves on to the next option.

"You should do a ritual to hear her."

"I don't like trucking with the dead," I say. "The cost is always too high."

"You mean the sacrifice?"

Pretty much all necromancy involves a sacrifice of some kind. The kid was able to get away with things because he sacrificed his soul. But for those of us who have magic that *doesn't* come from demons, something is going to have to die. I could use my own life force, cutting my days a bit shorter, or making me sick, or some shit like that. Or I could kill some mice, a rabbit, or some other cute animal that doesn't deserve to die.

I can minimize the cost, spend a few hours writing the proper glyphs and spells, but at the end of the day, something's gotta die. So thanks, but no thanks.

"I don't kill for fun," I say. I technically do kill for profit, but that's mostly to help the world be a better and safer place, so I'm giving myself a pass on that.

Stewart nods. "That is one of the things I like about you, Ashley."

"AJ," I correct him, though I know by now it won't really help. He'll still call me Ashley no matter how many times I tell him that I hate my name. *But it's so pretty.* Go fuck yourself.

He smiles, then puts a folder on his desk between us. "There is something that I needed to talk to you about, and it is not just the child necromancer."

"What is it then?"

"There has been a bit of an influx in magical energy lately."

"How much of an influx?"

"Last year's estimate was that there were ninety-seven witches above Threshold power in the twin cities." Threshold power means they are able to actually affect the world, not just put on a pretty show. "I had them run the tally again last week, and according to the results, there are three hundred and seventy-two witches above Threshold power."

I let out a whistle. That's not a coincidence. A rise or drop of five or so, that's a coincidence. Twenty is a trend. Three hundred? That's just fucked up.

"Where did they all come from?"

"That is the crux of it," he says. "I am not sure that anyone has moved into the territory, at least not more than one would normally expect. But the fact remains: the magic is more intense."

"Could it be a wizard?"

He shakes his head. "We cannot register their power."

I hate wizards. Think they're so smart just because the universe bends to their insanity.

"So either everyone in the city has gotten three times as powerful, or there are a whole lot of people suddenly getting Threshold level abilities."

"Precisely. I am sure you understand why this could be a problem."

It's one thing I don't like about my job. I tell myself that I'm getting the bad ones off the street, that I'm making the world better. But sometimes, I'm just keeping the balance. If one group starts to get too strong, then a whole lot more of their crimes suddenly carry death sentences. With this many witches in town, we're talking open season—jaywalkers might find themselves getting axed.

"Who knows about it?"

"Just you and me" he says. "And Jerome, who did the measuring. He is currently double checking in case it's a fluke. I predict you have as much as three days before he finishes and reports his findings to the council."

Three days before witchcraft becomes an extreme sport. Awesome.

"You think this has anything to do with the demons? Are they buying up souls and giving out magic?"

"It is possible. That would be against their rules to do on such a scale, but they are not always known to follow rules." He rubs his temple. "Whatever it is, Ashley, it needs to be taken care of. This large of an increase is not just unbalancing. It will be taken as a declaration of war."

Fuck. That's way worse. Too many witches means harsher punishment for crime. Declaration of war means a Culling—it means open season on witches. Like me.

"And you want me to find out why it's happening?"

He nods. "And put a stop to it, if you can. At the very least, having an explanation could stop anyone from making rash decisions too quickly. But if they find out about the spike, without knowing that the cause was unintentional—" he gives me a hard look, "and my expectation is that it *was* unintentional—without knowing that, drastic measures are likely to be taken."

That's more than a bit of a threat. Stewart isn't a witch. If even he thinks we're planning a war, then we may just be fucked.

"I'll see what I can find out," I tell him.

"Hurry."

INTERLUDE SIX

Jason was a strict teacher. He told me I was his apprentice, and he expected a lot of me. There was a constant stream of assignments for me to do, books for me to read, and symbols to draw over and over and over again. Any time I showed interest in any new symbol, he would make me draw it a thousand times. He trained me to be ambidextrous, making me draw things five hundred times with each hand.

I'd always liked drawing, but Jason was teaching me a skill. He was teaching me to be precise, to draw perfectly straight lines, to make perfect circles, all freehand.

But I insisted on another tattoo, a way to bind my growing magic. That's how I ended up with the symbols down my arms.

I asked him to tie me down again, but he refused. He said that I needed to be able to control myself. And he told me that what he was doing was a spell, and spells don't work if they aren't completed. So if I move, if I make him stop, then I will have gone through that pain without gaining anything from it.

It felt like hours. He put a symbol on my elbows, at the joint of my shoulders, across my back, and over my spine. I couldn't tell you which one hurt the most. It all got kind of lost in a haze. I know I cried. I know I begged him to stop. But I also know that I didn't move. I had the discipline not to.

CHAPTER SEVEN

First step, I suppose, is to contact the over-coven. Lots of witches form covens—it's totally the 'in' thing to do these days—but the over-coven is like a miniature council, like our government. They supposedly make policies and even enforce some of our stricter laws. I don't know that I've ever actually seen that happen, but that's the theory.

Getting in to meet with them isn't going to be easy. I don't have a coven. None of them would take me. Which stung a bit, yeah. But since my magic is mostly bound inside me, what little I have left isn't enough to cross the Threshold, so they don't consider me a 'real' witch. I can cast runic magic and draw glyphs better than anyone else in the cities, but since I can't summon an elemental or levitate or turn invisible or some other power that frankly qualifies people more to be X-Men than witches, I don't get to join a coven.

And that kinda sucks. Covens are where the best training comes from. They're where the most knowledge is stored. It's a matter of status, not just in the sense of having respect, but in the sense of what you might get exposed to. I can do a lot with my magic, and I can put it in people's skin—something that, as far as I know, only three other people in the country can do—but at the end of the day, my bag of tricks is limited to what I can figure out on my own. Having a coven would let me learn new things. Like maybe how to circumvent my bindings a little bit and light a fucking cigarette with my mind.

Anyway. The normal way to get in touch with the over-coven is to talk to your coven leaders. One of them is on the over-coven, and they can always find a way to gather enough of the others to have a quorum and help you out. All official covens have one member on the over-coven. That's how it works.

But I have no chain of command to work up. I have to either find a coven and get them to tell me who their over-coven member is, luck onto an over-coven meeting, or do something drastic to get their attention.

I could blow up a building or something. That would get their attention. But it really wouldn't be the kind of attention I want. They wouldn't be all that likely to listen to me. I can't really say "yeah, sorry about the massive destruction, but I wanted to ask a question about whether or not we're planning to go to war." I think I'd probably get out more like "Yeah, sorry—gurgle gurgle gurgle" as they slit my throat or some shit.

So that method is out.

I know what I have to do, but I really don't want to do it. I have to go to one of the other witches I know, get them to go to their coven leader, and get to the over-coven that way. Problem is, the other witches I know are assholes.

I know them because of the coven I tried to join. Which, now that I think about it, was an awful lot like pledging a sorority. At least, I assume; I never did the pledging thing. I barely started the college thing. Anyway.

It was a bunch of mean girls, like from that movie about the mean girls who rule the school, only to get taken down by a newcomer who they try to make popular, only to have her get more popular than them and socially destroy them. What was that one called? Jawbreaker, I think. Or Clueless. Or Mean

Girls. Or Heathers. Whatever.

They were judgmental as hell, and it took all of a second for them to decide I wasn't 'coven material.' They looked at my tattoos, at my clothes, and at my hair (which at the time was green) and decided that I wasn't what they were looking for. Being able to claim that I didn't have the magical ability to join the coven was just an easy out for them.

Fucking bitches.

My only hope, really, is Fred. Fred applied the same time I did, and from what I understand, Fred managed to get in. He somehow put up with the cattiness, the political backstabbing, and the general bitch fest and got into the coven. He's still the lowest on the totem pole, but at least *he* got into a coven.

We haven't spoken in over a year; they don't exactly forbid it, but discussing magic outside the coven is 'frowned upon,' and they made it clear that talking to me at all qualified as discussing magic. I can only hope he still works the same place he used to.

Fred works at Wells Fargo. That's a bank, a much more respectable job than tattoo artist or bartender, though I'd argue that those two professions have a lot more in common with witchcraft than something that uses terms like 'subprime' and 'deductible.'

Not that I'm bitter.

As soon as I walk inside, there's someone there to ask me if they can help me. I'm not sure if that's their normal policy or if I was immediately flagged as a source of potential trouble. Probably not; I'm still wearing long sleeves, my hair is a natural color (not *my* natural color, but one that does exist in nature), and while I'm wearing jeans and combat boots, that doesn't scream criminal, I don't think. Maybe I'm just being over sensitive.

"I'm looking for Fred," I say. I don't know his last name. "I know he used to work here, but it's been a while, and—"

Apparently, he still works there, as the smiling guy in the pink shirt tells me to have a seat and that he'll go get Fred for me. So either my key to the coven world is on his way, or someone else named Fred works here.

The guy who comes out to get me looks just like the Fred I knew—good sign there. He's wearing one of those blue shirts with the white collar and cuffs, suspenders, and a power tie. I don't remember him looking like quite this much of a douchebag. He smiles at me, but only the lower half of his face moves. It's a practiced smile, a professional smile, not a friendly one.

"AJ, wasn't it?" he says, holding out a hand to me.

I shake his hand and feel a bit of a tingle. He's got some mojo working. Probably something to charm people with, something to give him a bit more of an edge selling things like mortgages or equity credit whatevers.

"That's right," I say. "I'm kind of surprised you recognize me."

"You mean without the green hair?" He chuckles. "You're more memorable than you think, AJ. Why don't we go back to my office and have a chat?"

He's all friendly, but something about him makes me wish I'd come in armed. I'm pretty sure I can take him in a fight regardless, but still, having a knife would make me feel better.

I follow him and go into the office he gestures to, taking a seat across from a cheap desk with an out of date computer on it. He closes the door with a kind of finality, then moves and sits down across from me in a much more comfortable chair. The smile is gone, and he tents his fingers, tapping them on his lower lip. "What do you want?" he asks.

"Glad to see you've got fond memories of me," I say. "Or has the rumor mill just managed to get you to hate me like everyone else?"

"I don't hate you, AJ," he says, though the tone begs to differ. "If anything, I pity you."

That makes me laugh, in an I'm-about-to-punch-someone

kind of way. "Pity?"

"You've got more power than any two witches I know," he says. "But you don't have the control to really use it. You've got less control than an epileptic monkey with ADHD."

That's kind of harsh. I mean, it's not all wrong—when my magic first manifested, it ended up turning everything around me into a pile of molten slag. My clothes, the parking space, my boyfriend, his car, all of it. That's why I bound the fire in the first place. I never really had to learn to control my magic; when it gets strong enough, I get another tattoo.

"I have more control than you think."

"Sure, casting rote spells. But you had to bind up your own power just to be able to function." If it's possible, his voice seems to sneer a bit. "It's no wonder covens won't take you. And before you ask, no. We won't reconsider you either. Not until your seven years are up."

Every seven years, I get the opportunity to apply again. Or rush, or whatever. Six more and I can try to be with that swell group of folks again. I can hardly wait.

"I'm not here to ask to be reconsidered," I say through clenched teeth. "I don't give a flying shit what you fuckers think about me or about my magic. I'm here on business." I pull out a blank card and put it on the desk between us.

To normal folk, it's blank. To someone who can see magic, it details my position with the council. It's like an investigator's license, a license to kill, and a badge all rolled up in one. It's fun to watch the blood drain from his face when he looks at it.

"Th-that's *you*?" he asks. He's probably referring to the rumors about me when I'm working. I don't answer him. Somehow, it's better for the rep if you don't confirm *or* deny. "Look, I wasn't doing any harm by it, just making things a bit less stressful, and—"

I hold up a hand. "I'm not here to arrest you, Fred. I don't really care about the piddling shit you're doing. Not yet, anyway.

But I have to talk to the over-coven, PDQ. There's bad shit going on, and if I don't fix it fast, we might be looking at a war."

I probably shouldn't have told him that.

"A w-war?"

I nod. In for a penny... "And possibly a Culling."

Mentally, I bet he's pissing his pants about now.

"Look, can you get me in touch with the over-coven or not?"

"I can't," he says, and I believe that he wishes he could. "I don't—I can't even petition them yet."

"Then can you point me to someone who can? I need to talk to them like, yesterday."

"There's Amber," he says. "Amber's in line for a leadership position. She can probably get you in touch with them."

Amber. Perfect. Queen bitch herself.

I roll my eyes. "Fine," I say. "Make the call, or whatever you do."

INTERLUDE SEVEN

After that, we started talking about wands.

I asked him if the wand would choose me, and if we were going to Ollivander's. He didn't know who that was, and I made fun of him for being old. The last book had just come out, and he hadn't even read the first one yet! He made me do pushups.

That was a thing that Jason did. I don't know if it was military training in his past, or just a way to get me to shut up for a while, but he would make me do pushups any time he got annoyed with me. At the time, I didn't understand why people complained about them. I didn't mind them at all. And he never gave me too many to do at any given time. Fifty was usually enough, and never more than two hundred.

That, apparently, is a lot. And it probably would have been before that last tattoo. But after the tattoo, it just wasn't difficult. Lifting my own weight was just *easy*.

"It's because of the tattoo," he told me. "You're about three times as strong as you should be."

"Then why am I doing pushups?"

"Because it's three times what you should be. So the stronger you get, the stronger you'll be."

"Why do I need to be stronger than most people?"

He smiled, somewhat sadly. "Because it's only stronger than most humans, not most people."

After I finished doing the hundred pushups he demanded for my Ollivander comment, he went back to telling me about wands. They're just focuses. Foci. Whatever the right word is.

"Not all witches use them," he told me. "But for our purposes, you're going to need one."

"So you're not going to tell me I'm a wizard, Harry?"

He still didn't get it. "You are *not* a wizard," he told me. "You're a witch. Like me."

"Isn't the male version called Warlock?"

He shook his head. "Warlocks are something else entirely. I'm a witch. Male witches are more rare than female, but there's no gender to the term."

"So I'm a witch, Harry?" I shook my head. "That doesn't sound nearly as cool."

Fifty pushups later, he started talking about the process of making a wand. It's apparently a major undertaking. One that I wasn't ready for, and one that, honestly, I never would be. "It takes so much power to be able to make them," he told me. "I can't do it either."

And that was when I first learned about the Threshold.

CHAPTER EIGHT

This time, I *am* going in armed. I've got a knife strapped to each forearm, a switchblade in my pocket, and a throwing knife on the inside of my belt, laying across my back. It's not what I wear when I'm working, but it's enough, should things get rough. If Amber isn't going to help me willingly, I'm going to invoke a few of the privileges I get working for the Office, and I'm gonna cut a bitch. There will be paperwork to fill out, and probably some hassle down the road, but it'll be worth it.

Fred made the appointment for me, which was nice of him. I'm pretty sure I wouldn't have gotten in the door if he hadn't. Amber works in one of the big towers downtown, not too far from Foshay. It's not the IDS—I have no idea what goes on in there, but it can't be anything good—but it is a noticeable part of the city skyline, a fact I'm sure Amber thinks makes her more important. The lobby of this building is bigger than my apartment complex. So much marble on the floors that they practically shine, and a big ass security desk with half a dozen monitors and a guard who looks distinctly less bored when I come in the door.

"Can I help you?" he asks, his tone suggesting that he wants to do anything but.

"I have an appointment with Amber Blake," I say.

He raises an eyebrow like he doesn't believe me. "And your name?"

"Ashley Grey," I say through gritted teeth. He picks up his phone and dials a number to check me out. Clearly, he doesn't want me going past him. If he tries to search me, I'm going to break his nose. If for no other reason than that he made me say my name.

I hate my name. Ash Grey? Funny, Mom and Dad. Really fucking funny. At least my sister Darien Grey only gets made fun of by the literate, and sometimes complimented by the Oscar Wilde fans. Oh, but why not go by my middle name? Great question. Why *wouldn't* I go by Jean? Jean Grey? Not like that's the name of a character from a comic book or anything. Some people's parents are hippies. Mine are nerds. They may have figured out my magical resonance and named me accordingly. But I think they were just nerds. And possibly high.

I'm almost growling by the time he gets off the line. "Take the elevator to the sixteenth floor," he says, pointing and spelling out directions like he thinks I might wander around randomly and put my grubby hands on things. I now want to do that, just out of spite. "Someone will be waiting for you and will take you the rest of the way."

When I get into the elevator, I smear my hands all over the mirrored walls, leaving streaks that someone is going to have to clean up. Someone who didn't do anything wrong. Fuck. Now I feel like a bitch.

Well, at least I didn't scribe in a glyph to make the mirrors extra brittle so someone leaning against them will make them crack. Maybe I'll do that on the way out.

The elevator moves pretty fast, almost like the whole building just wants to give me the bum's rush. I can come in, but it doesn't want me staying any longer than absolutely necessary. Maybe it's the fingerprints thing. I guess I deserve it.

The woman standing at the elevator with a clipboard in her hands has clearly been briefed about me. Either that or she has an expression that needs to redefine 'resting bitch face.' Her blonde hair is perfectly put up in a bun, tight enough to show off her roots, which are also blonde. She has thick-framed black glasses that look like cat eyes, and her lips are held in a tight, disapproving line. She's gotten a manicure lately, and her suit is probably more expensive than my car. Not that my car is worth all that much, but you get the point.

"You must be Ms. Grey," she says, in the same tone of voice you might use with someone when you realize that it was, in fact, *them* who stepped in the dog shit. "If you would be so kind as to follow me?"

I swallow my words before they can get out and say something about kindness that this bitch probably needs to hear, because I know those words will probably be followed by my forearm across her nose, which in turn would lead to her getting reconstructive surgery, which I'd probably have to pay for. Better just to keep quiet.

See that? I'm growing up. All mature and shit.

I'm taken to an office, clearly this woman's. There's a door on the opposite wall, which I imagine leads to Amber. The woman who fetched me tells me to sit and "Try not to touch anything." She doesn't offer me water, but I'm pretty sure she uses hand sanitizer as soon as she sits down. Not that we shook hands or anything.

Amber knows I'm here. Which makes the next twenty minutes more and more annoying. She knows I'm here, she knew I was coming. She's making me wait out of spite, and so that I know she's more important than me.

This is why I work in the tattoo business. No stupid mind games. Our mind games are fun.

She doesn't meet me at the door. After my wait has put me in the appropriate mindset (that I'm annoying her and wasting her time), but before I pull out a switchblade and start carving my initials into the chair, Amber's minion tells me to go right in.

Amber is on the phone. Or she's holding the phone to her ear and making proclamations to a dial tone in order to look more important. She gestures me to a chair in front of her desk. A single, lonely chair. It's not angled in towards the desk, but rather facing it straight on, like the person sitting there is being interrogated.

Once I sit down and the light of the sun hits my eyes, it just further intensifies the whole interrogation feeling.

I brush my hair away from my septagram and take a look around. There's magic, but nothing all that spectacular. It's understated, little things like a pleasant fragrance to the air or temperature control way beyond what a thermostat can do. Nothing illegal. Nothing even *questionable*. It's all above board.

I wonder if she changed that for me.

I don't bother listening to her conversation, instead turning my gaze on her. That ring is enchanted. If I had to guess, it's defending her from others trying to read her mind or breach her aura. The necklace is also enchanted, though I can't tell how. I think her hair pin is enchanted too, likely with something dangerous.

Magic takes time, usually. You can sling it around in a pinch if you have to, but that's wild, uncontrolled, and dangerous as hell. You might burn yourself out doing that. So most of the really good witches put their power into objects a little at a time, building up the energy either to draw on later or just to use the object for a predetermined effect. Like magic wands, or rings of protection. Dungeons and Dragons got a surprising amount pretty dead on.

Amber puts the phone on its cradle and gives me a professional smile that seems like it's trying to melt my face off. "Ashley Grey," she says. "I didn't expect to hear from you for another five years and eleven months."

Fucking seven year rule.

"I'm not here about your little coven," I say, taking a bit of pride at the anger that flashes across her eyes when I call her coven little. "I'm here on a more official capacity." I hand her my blank card. She doesn't even glance at it.

"Yes, I've been informed. And you seem to think there is some kind of war brewing? Or did you just say that to give poor Fred a good scare? I do like your hair, by the way. Much more... professional."

It's never good to go into a viper den, and every conversation with Amber is a viper den. "Thanks," I say, waving away the back handed compliment. "I'm not trying to scare anyone. I just needed to impress the importance of me talking to the over-coven."

"For professional legal reasons, not to petition for anything." She says it as a statement.

I could in theory petition the over-coven to waive my seven year thing. I can demonstrate a lot more power than I seem to have; my bindings make it look like there's not much I can really do. But there's a big difference between not being able to power magic from within and not being able to do cool shit.

Does she really think I'm making shit up just so I can apply to her stupid sorority again?

"Listen Amber," I say. She puts her hands on her desk, folded like a teacher's pet, and smiles innocently. Suddenly, my angry tirade seems to be playing right into her trap. I let out a sigh. "Let me try this a different way. You know what I do, right? Fred told you." She nods. "So you know that if I wanted to, I could nitpick the hell out of your coven until you were all sanctioned one way or another, and no one would want to talk to you about joining, because they would know I was on your ass."

"That would be very vindictive of you. Is that a threat?"

"No," I say. "And it's not a promise. It's an observation. If I really gave even the smallest shit about you rejecting me, I have all kinds of powers I could abuse—legitimately—to fuck with you. I could be vindictive as hell. But I haven't been. And I'm not going to be. Because, and let me make this perfectly clear..." I lean forward to enunciate each word. "I. Don't. Care. About. You." I smile. "Or your coven. If any of you step out of line, I'll be there, but I'm not going out of my way looking for it. You just," I shrug, "you just don't matter enough to me."

She snorts. Derisively. She doesn't buy it. Like all popular kids, Amber thinks that everyone wants to be just like her, wants to be her friend.

Whatever.

"Just so long as we understand each other," she says. "This is not a petition."

I laugh. "It's not a fucking petition," I say. "It's an investigation. You're the fastest way I know to get in touch with the over-coven without making huge waves. I'm trying to be discreet."

She gives a laugh that is somehow more derisive than her snort. "*This* is you being discreet?" She gestures at me. "You walk into my place of business dressed like a street person, you rant on and on about nonsense threats and you demand that I bring you to the over-coven. And that is somehow discreet?"

I take a few deep breaths, willing my hand not to reach for a knife. Don't stab her. *Don't* stab her. *Don't stab her.*

"Yes," I say, my teeth and fists clenched.

"And what, dare I ask, would blunt look like?"

Oh, I'm so glad she asked. "Blunt would have been me knocking your secretary on her ass, breaking down your door, and then dangling you out the window until you gave me the information that I need. Blunt would be drawing hexes on the outside of your building and making your electricity fail until you told me what I needed to know. Blunt would be me raining hell down on every aspect of your life for a few days before even *asking* for the information." I shrug, then crack my neck. "Of course, if you'd rather do blunt, I can do that. Your call."

She frowns at me, fiercely. Once more trying to get my face to melt off. I really wish she would just sling some fire at me. Then I could bust her ass and have a really fun time of making her resist arrest.

I'm not usually like this, I promise. But this bitch is pushing me.

She takes a sticky note and a pen and writes something down, barely looking at it. She hands me the note. "Their next meeting is tonight at this address. When the clock strikes midnight. If you can get inside, you can feel free to talk to one of them the way you talked to me. We'll see how well that goes for you."

I take the paper from her. "Go fuck yourself, Amber," I say. "You're lucky I'm walking out of here without breaking your nose first."

"That sounded like a threat. I could have you charged for assault."

I shake my head and stand up. "No you couldn't. But if you want to try, be my guest."

She has to get the last word in, just as I reach the door. "It's not wise to upset a coven when you have none to protect you," she says.

Now *that* was a threat.

I mollify myself by pressing the button for every floor right before getting off the elevator. It may be childish, but it makes me feel better.

I have some time to kill before the over-coven meeting. Time enough to grab a slice of pizza from that New York Pizza place. I know Midwesterners aren't supposed to like East coast pizza, but NYC does it right. Greasy, delicious, foldable. And they call it soda, not pop. Being native to Chicago, I will be killed if I ever admit it out loud. But deep dish is just, you know, too much.

While I'm sitting at a table with the red and white squares, those colors that are supposed to make you hungry, I can't help but wonder what the hell I'm going to say to the over-coven. They probably don't know me, but they'll know all *about* me from Amber before I show up. So I should go in expected to be treated like dirt, or at best like a deranged monkey with a knife. It's going to be hard to get them to take my word for pretty much anything.

Maybe I *should* join a coven. Then I'd have some sort of status in the witch world. I can prove to a coven that I meet the Threshold. I can prove that I can do more than most. I just need the opportunity.

And the right people. If I have to join a coven, it needs to be full of cool people. Not jet-setters and VIP table people, just people who won't treat me like a second-class witch because I can't sling it around freestyle. People who won't hold my childhood lack of control against me.

I like to think I've gotten better. I mean, it takes a lot of self-control to tattoo. You have to keep your hand steady, you have to pay enough attention to lift the needle before the client starts to twitch or pull away, and you need to focus on this little drawing for hours at a time. And magical tattoos are a whole different story. Those have to be done old style, and by hand. They have to be done with incredible precision, and the clients are going to be in a lot of pain. I have to focus the whole time I'm doing it, sending in energy to bind the ink to the magic to the person. And I have to do it all in one sitting. You can't stop a spell halfway through just because you want a cigarette.

And then there's the screaming and the crying. Most people do one or the other. I don't blame them. It feels like I'm gouging out their skin with a rusty spoon, or like I'm setting their pubic hair on fire at the roots. I've also heard it described as being like slamming your fingers in a car door, non-stop, for hours. I like the battery acid analogy myself. It's always felt like my skin is being burned away, like my flesh is melting off.

And for the record, I cry. Every time. You think you'll get used to it, but you won't.

My first one, the one that bound in my fire, Jason had to tie me down to do it. And I mean that literally. I wonder if that's where the whole bondage thing started. Not important.

What matters is that years of tattooing, both mundane and magical, have given me a hell of a lot more control, and I should be able to get into a coven if I want to. I mean, control is control, right? Being able to keep my hand steady while I draw on someone's flesh is the same as controlling your magic, right? I mean, probably. I'm sure it would be fine.

All I'd really have to do is find a coven I wouldn't mind being a member of.

I've given myself this pep talk before. And I always start to feel like the covens are bitchy sororities. I always psych myself out, convince myself that I wouldn't want to be part of it anyway, so I'm more bitter than disappointed when they say no. And so far, all of them have. I haven't tried every coven in the cities, of course. My ego couldn't take any more rejection after number five. I'm not third time lucky. Even my safety covens said no.

I sigh and stick a bunch of pizza in my mouth, biting down and chewing the deliciously greasy slice of heaven as I try to focus on the now, on tonight. If I were part of a coven, that would make it easier, sure. But I'm not. So what the fuck am I supposed to do?

Do I raise the issue subtly? Do I ask if there's been an influx of witches? Do I ask if we've been lying on the census? Maybe I could just tell them that there is worry that the witches won't be strong enough for something, and see if they laugh at me. I could go the subtle route.

But I won't. Knowing me, and I do, I'll be as blunt as a club to the knee.

INTERLUDE EIGHT

The Threshold.

With witches, there's a way of seeing how much power someone has. I said that my parents weren't witches. Technically, that's not true. They do have a tiny bit of magic, it just isn't enough for them to ever really do anything with it. But my dad never gets caught at a red light for long, and my mom's garden grows better than any of the other gardens on the block. That's about it.

As a witch grows in power, they come close to the point where they can do certain things. Things like building a wand, or casting spells on the fly, making potions, all that kind of stuff. That point is called the Threshold. Being able to cross it is kind of a prerequisite for being a part of witch society.

The trouble is that my tattoos were binding my magic. I barely registered as a witch at all with just the two tattoos. I could still use it, but my natural power was pretty much zero.

I didn't care at the time. I *wanted* my magic bound. I could still see Geoff's face when I closed my eyes for too long, and still heard his mother calling me a murderer when I slept.

The point is, it takes someone way beyond the Threshold to be able to make a wand. Thankfully, there are people out there who make them for those of us who can't use them. Jason got me mine. It's a nice piece of rosewood, covered with so many carvings they're almost impossible to make out. But when I looked really closely at it, I could make out every symbol. I could understand the whole thing, though it would take several pages to actually write down all the symbols, and that's if I kept them small.

There weren't any special effects when I first touched the wand. Turns out, they're not unique to one user. The longer you use it, the better it will work for you and with your magic.

But that's true of fountain pens too.

CHAPTER NINE

I take off the hoodie before I go in. It's not a matter of hoodies being unprofessional. And it's not a matter of heat—I don't really feel temperatures, remember? So wearing a tank top when it's only twenty degrees outside doesn't bother me. But it does send a message. Lots of them, in fact.

I want them to see my arms. They'll look at me with special sight, and they'll see the actual sigils there. They'll see past the key on my wrist and see the unbinding spell. They'll look past the black swirls and see the spells I have woven into my arms. They'll see the ankh, the beginnings of the slash, and they'll see the protection spells woven underneath them. They'll look at my hands, and—well, they probably won't be close enough to make out what's actually there, but they will get the impression that there are spells there.

Hopefully, they'll understand that I am prepared for a fight, but that I didn't bring any weapons with me. I want to be a bit intimidating, but not threatening. And I want them to wonder what I have covered up by my pants, my boots, and my tank top.

There's no one at the door, no guard, no bouncer. There doesn't need to be. Without the septagram showing me where it is, I couldn't possibly have found this place. It's not technically invisible, but it's one of those things where you'll always drive past it, or you'll get distracted by something and look away. The mailman can't seem to find this address. And forget about food delivery. Basically, a much more powerful version of the one on my apartment door.

Not that it matters; this isn't a residence. And the warding that pulls attention away is fresh. Probably bound to the night. At sunrise, it'll all just float away into the ether. Those sorts of things are way easier to do, and doing them at an over-coven meeting sends a very clear message: they don't meet in the same place twice.

So once I find the door, all I have to deal with is the pressure spell keeping it closed. Again, it's not that bad. Probably four or five hundred pounds of pressure will get through it. Virtually any witch worth their salt can let out a force bolt that strong.

And me? Well, I can just apply the necessary pressure. I'm stronger than I look. (I'm stronger than any human looks). Not to say it opens easily, but it does open. I do get through.

And I ignore the illusions of emptiness, or of fire, or whatever last line of defense they have thrown up. It's probably only half assed anyway—three lines of defense is more tradition than necessity. It's not like anyone's going to crash a meeting of the most powerful witches in the area. Or like they'll survive if they do it.

That does not bode well for me.

Thirteen members of the over-coven are staring at me as I walk in. Some of them, I'm sure, are looking at the spells woven through me. Some of them recognize me. Some of them just seem bored. If they're bored at meetings, maybe I should talk to them about a coven membership. I'll bet I could make meetings more exciting.

"Neophyte Grey," says the one in the chair directly opposite the door. I guess that makes him the one in charge. He's wearing a nice suit, well-tailored but subtle, the colors muted in the classiest way possible.

I try not to give him the finger at calling me a neophyte. I'm not in a coven, so technically he's correct. Never mind that neophytes could never have made it through the door.

"You've been told I was coming tonight?" I ask.

Guy in charge nods. "Yes we were. Adept Blake informed us of your," he pauses, filling the next word with venom, "request."

I walk deeper into the room like there's nothing to worry about. I even go inside their circle of chairs. Never mind what they could do to me if they wanted to. Never let them see you sweat, or let them think they have you scared. Always act like you've got an ace in the hole. Or, in this case, a tactical nuclear strike primed and ready to launch on your say-so.

"So I don't have to waste time telling you in what capacity I'm here." I nod and cross my arms. "Good." Arms crossed feels like a bad idea. But putting them in my pockets would be worse, and I'd feel weird with them just hanging there. Folded in front of me is out, and behind my back might send the wrong message. Fuck it. "And in that capacity, I have a few questions I need to ask."

Guy in charge raises an eyebrow. I've been talking to him pretty directly, so I think I know what he's about to say. "Questions for me specifically?" he asks.

Yep, that's what I thought. "Questions for the over-coven," I assure him, taking the time to glance around and at least pretend to make some eye contact. "It's about a matter that affects our people through the cities, and this was the fastest way I could get the information I need."

"And what information *do* you 'need'?" This comes from a blonde Norse-looking woman. I know her—she's in Amber's coven. What's her name? Bitch? No, that's just what everyone calls her. I think her name is Laura Svongaard or some shit like that. The air quotes just make me want to call her bitch, though. Or worse.

I stare at her, locking eyes so she's certain I'm not afraid. I feel like a wolf fighting for dominance. But that's how it feels in coven sororities. "I need to know if there has been a sudden and massive influx of our kind in the city," I say. "And I need to know if we—if *you*—are planning on going to war."

They seem confused when I start, annoyed as I continue, and then shocked at the last word. The shock seems genuine, so I can probably rule that one out. Good; if they were going to war, I don't know how I could stop them.

There's chattering for a few seconds, people leaning over and having little mini conferences. I lean back on my heels a bit and decide that the arms crossed was probably the right way to go after all.

Guy in charge shuts everyone up pretty quickly, though. "Why would you, in your official capacity, be asking these questions?"

That's not a no. And it's not a yes. Fucking politics. "The Threshold census," I say. No point in hiding things. "According to a new test performed a few days ago, there are more than three hundred and seventy of us." I don't need to say the rest of it, but I do. "That's a pretty significant increase. So I need to know: is it an increase in power or an increase in numbers?"

Three hundred and seventy-two witches at Threshold power doesn't necessarily mean that many new witches. It could mean that some people have increased in power, or that there are people who rank far enough above the Threshold to skew the results. Without my ink, I know I'd rank as about three witches. With it, I don't even rank as one.

Most of the people in here rank as at least two. Some as many as four. And, if guy in charge is who I think he is, at least one of them ranks as five.

"That would be a pretty massive increase, either way," guy in charge says. "How sure are you that this information is accurate?"

"Sure enough that my boss sent me to figure things out before it goes public," I say. "He wants to avoid a war, and he's pretty sure that's what'll happen if we don't have a damned good explanation for him. That or a Culling."

Cullings are bad. Cullings involve lots of people either leaving the area or leaving this mortal coil.

Guy in charge stays calm while everyone else freaks out. "We will have to investigate this ourselves and get back to you, Neophyte Grey," he says, his voice carrying over a pretty raucous tumult of arguing, accusing, denying, and other politic type stuff. "I will have an answer for you very shortly. For now, you may go."

Ah, dismissal. If I wasn't so eager to get out of here and go home, I'd be annoyed. I mean, I *am* annoyed; they really didn't give me any information. But I can understand that it takes a while to figure this out.

I just hope it doesn't take too long.

"Clock's ticking," I say, spinning on my toes and walking out, glad I could get in the last word.

INTERLUDE NINE

Jason had me make a box for my wand. I had to craft it myself, and he made me put all kinds of sigils and symbols on it. Of course, he made me draw them a thousand times each before he let me even sketch them onto the wood. Then he lashed an exacto blade to my wand and made me practice cutting symbols into other wood (not the box) for a week before letting me actually carve the box. It was annoying, but I understood why just a few weeks later.

Magical sight is a weird thing. I had gained it a few months after my first tattoo, but lost it again when I got the second one. It came back, though, and I learned how to unfocus my eyes just the right way, letting me see the currents and threads of the magical world. Apparently, everyone sees this stuff differently. That's because it's not really "sight"; it's just how our brains interpret the information. Some people see auras. Some hear music or even smell different aromas. I see strings that vibrate. I blame physics.

Anyway, when I looked at the box I had made, I saw that it was siphoning magic from the air. Just a bit at a time. It was like the box was a turbine, and the magic was the wind blowing through it. It didn't actually change anything, but it did charge the hell out of the box. Or, rather, it charged the wand inside.

We worked on my wand. He had me ask my parents for some old family silver. My mom sent us her father's wedding band, and my dad sent his mother's hatpin. We melted them both down and made three silver needles. These Jason had me lash to my wand, the three points coming together and crossing each other. I lashed it first with twine, then again with wire. He had me burn off the twine. Then we covered the lashing with natural clay. I held it, and my hand, in a fire for several minutes to make sure that it dried right. Then I smashed the clay. Then we lashed the needles on with animal gut. Once that happened, I cut the wire off. And then he gave me something that made me feel a bit gross.

It was a long strand of sinew. And it was human. I lashed the needles down with it, and managed to avoid vomiting, but it was a close thing. Mostly I tried to focus on anything but the question of where he got the sinew. I did it, and when I was done, Jason announced my wand complete.

"The point of this is that you can get a bit away from the symbols themselves," he tells me. "It's easiest to use established symbols and sigils, because there is already power in those. But when you can't do that—maybe there isn't enough space, or something like that—then you use the magic in the wand. Between that and the right ink, you can make your own symbol, or use some other symbol for a different meaning."

When he showed me what he meant, we did it by tattooing a septagram at the edge of my scalp. My hair was just starting to grow out of that horrible mullet phase, so I could actually push the hair out of the way if I wanted to. And that became the point. We wanted the septagram to be able to work, but only when it wasn't covered. After that, I didn't need to refocus my eyes to see the magic; all I had to do was brush my hair behind my ears.

CHAPTER TEN

The first thing I do when I get home is pour myself a very large drink. Hello there, very large drink. My nerves are a bit frayed, and I'm fucking exhausted. I don't usually get up until eleven, so today's early morning was hard enough. Dealing with Amber and her coven bullshit didn't make it any easier.

So it's been a long day. On the plus side, I'm no closer to figuring anything out or solving anything than I was when I dragged my ass out of bed. Hello again, very large drink.

One of the biggest problems with working as a supernatural cop, or whatever it is I do, is that I still have a day job. And even if the world is on the brink of ending, I still have to pay the bills. My landlord isn't going to accept "but I was saving the world" as a good excuse for my rent being late.

It would be different if the Office job paid better. Or paid regularly. Or paid cash. I don't get paid until and unless I solve a problem. Which means until I've settled this whole thing, Stewart isn't likely to cut me a check. Then again, he might not even pay me in human currency. I might get some neat stuff, but neat stuff like power crystals or angel blood or Oni horn doesn't pay the bills.

Tattoos pay the bills. Tattoos pay cash.

And according to that neat little app on my phone that keeps track of that sort of thing, I have to work in the morning. Well, not *morning*. I have appointments at noon, three, and six. Not so bad. If I remember right, only one of them is going to take the full three hours. So I should have time for some lunch, and maybe some snooping, while I work. Then I'll go to the gym for a bit, and by then maybe the over-coven will have gotten back to me.

But in the meantime, back to my very large drink.

Hi.

INTERLUDE TEN

I don't know how long an apprenticeship is supposed to go, but Jason kept me working for about a year. I was spending hours drawing every day, getting things precise and smooth. But also drawing other things, giving more focus to creating an image that contains a spell than just drawing wards and sigils. I probably spent eighty hours a week working on my magic, not really learning much of anything else. I didn't have any connection with other witches, never really got into the local politics, because Jason didn't.

They say it takes 10,000 hours to be an expert at something. Eighty hours a week is only about four thousand. That plus the time I had spent working before being Jason's apprentice still only got me about halfway to the goal.

But Jason insisted that was okay. Five thousand hours is still a lot. It's still a certain level of expertise. And I was precise, which really impressed him. Enough that he decided to give me a final exam.

I had a month to prepare for it, but he wanted wings. I'd seen a ton of wing tattoos. I really like them, even if they are cliché. But he wanted more than just a picture of wings. He wanted them to function. He wanted to be able to fly, at least a little.

It would take a lot of power from him to bind wings that would actually work. He told me he hasn't gotten a new tattoo in years, and that he thinks he has the power that can do it. But just in case, I designed the wings to draw on his available power, rather than just bind it. So maybe it would let him glide. Maybe it would make him fly. Maybe it would just stop him from falling too hard.

I had to bind *some* magic into it. At the very least, I needed to stop him from falling too hard. That was part of the test. We were going to go skydiving when the tat was finished. And then he was going to rely on his wings to get him safely to the ground.

"I mean, I'll have a parachute too. I'm not stupid. But if I have to use it, or if it auto deploys, you fail your test. Fair?"

I didn't know why it would auto deploy; apparently, that's a thing that happens if you drop below a certain height while going faster than a certain speed. So my test was in two parts: first, to see if I could design the tattoo correctly and cast the spell, and to see how well it worked when it was finished.

I drew a set of wings with symbols drawn into the feathers. I covered every eventuality I could. I made sure that it didn't draw energy from his body, so his body temperature wouldn't drop to dangerous levels. I focused the wings more on removing the pull of gravity than on making him fly. It's close to the same thing. I also put some avian runes in there, stuff to suggest that he might be able to glide.

It took me three days to pick the right symbols, another two to draw it out, then three weeks of drawing it again and again to make sure everything was perfect. I did not want to screw this up. I then spent several days making the ink, burning bird bones and grinding up the charred remains, boiling down dove blood and mixing it with the char, then wrapping that with hawk feathers and burning the result. That char gave me the base for the black ink we would be using. It may have been overboard, but I wanted to be sure.

CHAPTER ELEVEN

My first client is a no show. Those piss me off. Not just because I could've had someone else to work on, but because of how much time I spent with the design. People don't seem to realize that the actual needle work is only a small fraction of the tattoo. Drawing it up, making sure the client likes it, making sure it'll fit on the skin, all that takes time. So no, I won't sketch something up for you. Not until you make an appointment.

And that's why we have deposits. To pay for our time if you flake out. So great, I made fifty bucks for some drawing. Would've made three times that if the jackass had showed up, and that's even with the shop fees.

Then again, maybe I'll get lucky and get a walk in. Walk ins are how you get new clients, and everyone can use new clients.

So I sit up towards the front of the shop, ready to pounce on anyone who comes in, and spend my time drawing to get ready for my appointments later. This Aztec elephant is gonna look badass.

I can't focus on it too long, though, before something else floats into my mind. Michelle. The poor dead girl who can't move on until I help her. Only, I don't know how to help her. I don't know what she needs.

So I guess I'll look like a crazy woman.

I pull my hair away from the septagram and look around until I spot her. She's just standing there, staring out the window.

"Michelle?" I ask. She turns and looks at me, her eyes starting to fill with hope. I point across the table and push one of the chairs out a little bit with my foot. "Can you sit down so we can talk?"

Ghosts can't really interact with the physical world. Hence the whole walking through walls thing. But they can settle down on anything they think is solid. That's why they don't fall through the floor. So Michelle can't move the chair out, but she can sit on it just fine.

"Here's the problem," I say. "I can't hear you. And you don't speak sign language."

She shakes her head and says something. I'm guessing it's that she can't sign, but I picked that up when we first met. Maybe her memory is starting to fade. That's bad. The soul fire did a real number on her. Hopefully I can remind her a bit, keep her sane for a bit longer.

"You can't write anything down, so that really limits how we can communicate. Mostly, I think we're stuck with yes and no."

She nods, then starts to say something but stops, looking embarrassed.

I chuckle. "It's okay to talk still. I can't hear you, but *you* can hear you, and sometimes it helps to hear your own voice. Might even help us figure things out." I set aside my drawing and bring out a blank piece of paper, just in case we come up with something good.

"Let's start simple," I say. "Were you murdered?"

She shakes her head no. Hey, one for the win column.

"Okay, good. Was your death violent?" Another no. "But you have something you have to do, something involved with your necklace." I've put it around my own neck for safe keeping. It's weird wearing a cross, but it's not like it's uncomfortable.

She nods and says something. She talks with her hands, which is good, but just random gestures, which isn't helpful.

"Does it belong to someone else?" She shakes her head. "Should it?" A nod. "Parent?" No. "Child?" She says something that looks like she's offended that I would even ask something like that. She was seventeen, though, and while it doesn't happen all the time, it *does* happen. "Sibling?" Still no. "Boyfriend?" Another no, combined with a rolling of the eyes and another sentence said in a bit of a huff.

Of course.

"Girlfriend?"

She puts one finger on her nose and points the other at me, nodding excitedly.

"Okay, so the necklace needs to go to your girlfriend. I don't suppose your family knows her name?"

She says something and shakes her head. I'm guessing she was still in the closet.

Well, I could go through a list of high schools until we find Michelle's—gonna have to do that anyway—then go there and let her point the girl out to me. That would be the easy way, and the way it would've been done twenty years ago. But today? A woman in her twenties, covered in tattoos, literally scoping out the high school girls? Not as bad as if I were a guy, but still pretty bad.

And Michelle can't very well tell me her name. Or draw me a picture. Ooh, there's a thought.

"Any chance your girlfriend's picture would be in a yearbook?" She nods and claps her hands, which I can't hear. "Okay," I say. "We'll go by the school and see if I can get my hands on an old yearbook. But it's going to have to be tomorrow. Can you hold it together a little longer?"

She nods.

Someone comes in the front door. I give Michelle an

apologetic look and stand up to go talk to them.

"Hey there, welcome to Inkspot. Do you have an appointment, or is there something I can do for you?"

There are other artists here. Most of them are off today, though. Which is probably a good thing, I realize, as soon as the someone speaks up.

"Yesss," he says, and I get a good look at him. His face is scaly, he has no nose, and his tongue is forked. Looks like he has a hoodie to hide things with, but there's no way this guy is going to pass for human. "I wasss hoping to find the one called AJ." He looks at me, his tongue flicking out for a second. "I'm assssuming that'ss you," he says. "You're ssstill ssstanding there, not running off to hide." The way he says it is apologetic, not threatening. Like he hates that people do that, and wants them to stop. Maybe that's just it.

"Yeah," I say, "that's me. What are you looking to get?"

He reaches into a pocket and pulls out a crumpled wad of cash. I see both a twenty and a fifty, along with a bunch of other bills. None of them are bloodstained. That's important, if only because it means he probably didn't kill anyone for it. "Is this enough for you to hide my—" He gestures to his face with a scaly and clawed hand. "I jussst want to look human again."

Ahh. Again. That makes sense.

I smile. "I can. I can even help with the lisp, at least to other people's ears, if you want. Do you by any chance have a picture? Of yourself, I mean."

He pulls a driver's license from his other pocket. He wasn't exactly bad looking, but not a prize winner either. He puts the pile of money down on the table and starts sorting it out.

"I have eight hundred," he says. "Will that be enough?"

I smile at him. "Since you didn't ask if it would 'ssssuficce,'" I say, affecting an over the top snake voice, "we should be able to do it for half that."

He smiles, looking relieved. A smiling snake creature is not reassuring.

"Why don't you go back and have a seat," I say, pointing to my station. "I'll see what I can draw up."

He nods his thanks and heads off. At least he's still walking on two feet. That'll make it easier. If he was slithering, it would be a whole different spell.

He wants an illusion. But a mostly static one. It'll move, but I can attach it to his body, so it moves when and how he does. That's not really that hard.

Getting the illusion to look like his old self, though, is a bit more complicated.

If I wanted to just hide him, I could put a few obscuring symbols together and just make sure no one really *noticed* the snake thing; that was my plan for the speech thing. But to actually make him look like a specific person is tough.

Thankfully, the license is an old one, and it looks pretty worn. He's kept it close to him, kind of a comfort. That means he's put a lot of attachment into it. That'll help.

Realistically, I should be taking his whole eight hundred. But something tells me it's all the money he has in the world, and I don't want to do that to him. This money isn't going on the books anyway, and I won't be paying the shop fee—since I'll be using my own equipment and ink—so four hundred is still a pretty solid chunk of change, even if it's less than this is worth.

I draw a celtic binding symbol on the back of the license, and an identical symbol on the tracing paper. It's a fae sign, and they're big with illusions and glamour. And this is basically just a glamour. But it'll be specific. So I surround the symbol with a Norse rune for man. I put a kanji for self at the bottom, closing off the square around the original symbol. Then I need one for speech, one for sound, and one for permanence. I stick with kanji for all three, surrounding the square and making a design that really isn't all that unpleasant to look at.

I needed the permanence so that it won't turn off every time he covers it up, like the way my septagram works. I should check and make sure he's okay with the permanence, though.

I run the paper through the machine that makes the actual stencil and bring it back to him. "Is it okay if this is permanent?" I ask. "Like, you'll never look like you do now again."

He smiles and closes his eyes. "That," he says, "would be delightful."

Okay then. Now for the delicate part. "I'm going to have to destroy your license to do this," I say. "I hope that's okay." He nods. I sigh. "Okay, I'm going to get this prepped, you figure out where you want the symbol. It'll still be visible with human skin, so pick carefully. And yes, this is going to hurt. A lot." I put on a pair of latex gloves and wait for him to nod. Once he's done that, I can move on.

I pull a box from under my station. It's made of solid black wood, and pretty fucking heavy. Carved into every surface of the box are various symbols of protection and a few of feeding and storage. It literally pulls magical energy out of the world around it and suffuses it into the contents. Not dangerous, but important.

Inside there is a set of bowls that were originally meant to be used for sake. They've got runes on them too, all five of them. I don't need Japanese elements, don't need Aristotelian elements. I need—that's the one. It's more modern, and it includes plastic.

I put the license in the little bowl and pull out my lighter. This is going to stink, but not for long. Once I start the license burning, the bowl takes over. In a quick flash, the license is gone, and only a fine powder remains. Ash.

I take a little cup from the shop and fill it halfway with black ink, then pour in the ash, getting as much as I can in there. Then I get out my stick.

It's the closest thing I have to a magic wand. It's about the right length, made of rosewood, and carved all over with various symbols. I didn't make it; I honestly don't know what half the symbols on it are, and I have no fucking clue how they were made so small and so precise.

Unlike Harry Potter's wand, though, mine has three needles at one tip. Three silver needles, lashed in place by human sinew. That used to gross me out. But I made it a long time ago, and that feeling has long since faded.

I use the needles to stir the ash into the ink. It doesn't take long. Once the needles are in there, the spell starts.

I set the stick down, needles still resting on the side of the little plastic cup, and throw out my gloves.

Then I look at him again. "Okay," I say. "Are you ready?"

He nods and rolls up his sleeve, then points at his forearm. It's scaly, no surprise there, and slightly greenish. "Here," he says.

I smear a bit of the goo on his arm, then lay the stencil against his skin and give it a good rub. When I peel the paper away, the symbol is hard to see, but definitely there.

"Normally," I say, "you'd have to sign consent forms and all that, and then we'd have a nice chat. But this isn't a normal situation. Once I start, I can't stop. And it's going to be incredibly painful. If you want, I can chain you to the chair." I have lots of bondage toys. It wasn't a big deal to sacrifice a few of them to help make this part easier.

He shakes his head. "I'll be fine," he says.

"Don't say I didn't warn you," I say. "And try not to scream too loudly."

I put my hair back, pulling it away from the septagram, and tie it off. I might not be able to see the design with the naked eye, but it has a faint glow to my magical sight. Like I said, the spell has already begun.

I put on a fresh pair of gloves and pick up my stick. One hand clamps down on his wrist to hold him steady, the other gets ready to start.

From the first strike, I know he was underestimating the pain. Like most others, he tries to pull away from me. It's a natural reaction. Oddly enough, it was that reaction that made me put the strength spell on my arms. He's only got human strength, thankfully, so he's not moving that arm until I let him.

I work as fast as I can, but I have to make sure to be precise. Wouldn't want to put him through all this pain and have it not work.

I can hear his muffled whimpers, and a quick glance shows me that he has his other hand over his mouth, his eyes clenched shut against the pain. Good man.

I can see the effect start to take hold as I move through it. He hazes a bit around the edges, the symbols become clearer and the image of humanity seeming to flow out of it. I use my magical sight to tell where the spell is going, what needs to be done, and how to finish it off.

By the time I finish, his muffled screams have turned to moans and whimpers. When I finally stop, he takes a deep, shuddering breath, letting it out slowly. Then he takes another breath, stronger this time. His eyes still haven't opened.

I smear bacitracin over what looks like normal human skin. "Do you want to take a look before I bandage it?" I ask, a little bit of a smile in my voice.

He opens his eyes one at a time, as if afraid of what he's going to see. But by the time he realizes what he's seeing, I almost need to lever him back into the chair. "Amazing!" he says. "It looks— It looks—" He spots one of the many mirrors, and his free hand goes to touch his face. "It's me." His voice is filled with awe, and there's a tear in his eye. Not one of pain.

I put a bandage over the tattoo and start wrapping a bandage around his arm. "I'm not entirely sure how you're going to heal," I say, "but keep it clean, put medication on it—I'll give you a sample packet of the stuff you need. You can get it at any drugstore."

"I'm human again," he says, his voice about to break.

"No," I say, pressing the bandage into place. "The only thing that's changed is appearance. If someone touches you, they'll feel your real skin. In your case, beauty isn't even skin deep."

"I don't care," he says. "I look like me again."

I toss my gloves in the trash and start cleaning my kit.

"Can I hug you?"

I laugh. "I appreciate the thought, but I'm not really a hugger."

He puts money into my hand and shakes it nice and firm. "Thank you," he says. "I can't thank you enough, really."

"Just keep what you really are a secret; that would be great."

I don't count the money until he's gone—that would be rude. He gave me six hundred. Cool. I do this sort of thing a lot; you'd think the Office would pay me for it.

Once my station is cleaned up, I go out to have a smoke. My box is back where it's supposed to be, and my station is as sterile as an operating room.

I walk halfway down the block before I light up. It's not that I care if people know that I'm associated with the shop or anything; I just don't want someone to have to walk through my cloud of smoke to get inside. And it's a good thing I do; while I'm out there, someone else walks in. One of the other artists will get that client. Which kinda sucks.

Six hundred bucks is great, but I'm never going to see him again. No way in hell is he going to want another of those tattoos just for fun. Magic doesn't bring regular clients. Walk-ins do, though.

I take a drag and try not to hate whoever ends up with that client. Better to focus on the case. Better to focus on what I know, or what I really, really don't.

The witches aren't planning to go to war. At least, the over-coven isn't. Stewart should be happy to hear that. But I don't have any kind of answer for what *is* going on. And just because the over-coven isn't planning for war doesn't mean that witches aren't going to war. It's possible that there's a group wanting to take over for the over-coven. An internal power struggle could bring in some serious numbers to an area. And while that means no one else is really in danger, it doesn't do much for the possibility of the Culling.

There needs to be an explanation for the rise in power that isn't numbers. If three hundred witches have just moved into town, there's going to be a problem, no matter how you slice it. But if it's something else—a change in how the test is given, a recategorization, a celestial event, even a massive increase in power could be better.

Well, massive increase in power across the board would probably still be bad.

And it's not like three hundred people *suddenly* gained enough power to cross the Threshold. Right?

I rub the cross hanging under my shirt, Michelle's cross. I really hope there's no connection. If there is, the demons will have hell to pay.

No pun intended.

INTERLUDE ELEVEN

The fact that Jason was giving me his whole back to tattoo was pretty amazing. I mean, if I screwed up, he would be sitting through all the pain for no reason. And he said it never stops hurting that much. Something about the magic binding into the flesh that is particularly painful. Makes sense to me, even if I don't understand the whole metaphysics of it.

He did ask me, several times, if I was ready to put the stencil on him. He wanted to make sure I was confident that I wouldn't ruin his skin. He wanted to be sure that the spell would work.

We did a trial run, where I just drew the entire design on his back with a Sharpie. It wasn't enough to actually do anything, but I was able to pull my hair aside and see that the magic worked. Marker isn't permanent enough for the magic to actually do what it's supposed to, but I could see as I worked that the energy was flowing through the right channels. There wasn't the energy to support it, but it was enough to be confident.

He put a mouth guard in before we started. He wanted to bite down, but didn't want to clench his jaw too much. Said it gave him headaches. I thought that was a good explanation for the various ball gags and other such things he had in his room. I suppose in a way it was: good enough, even if not correct.

He never screamed, but he did cry. I could see the tears flowing down his face, and could hear the whines of pain as I worked. But I didn't hurry. He was very clear on that. "It has to take as long as it takes," he said. "I'd rather you take ten hours to do it right than five hours and have you screw it up."

We set up with a lot of provisions. He was laying comfortably, and a friend of his even gave him an IV to keep him hydrated. I had half a dozen bottles of Gatorade and tea near at hand. He wasn't kidding about the length of time it would take to do this tattoo, and I couldn't take breaks. Even if he passed out, I couldn't stop.

I didn't know at the time, but that's a pretty big no-no in the world of tattooing. So is having a session that lasts more than a few hours. But that's tattoos, not spells.

Putting his wings on was a serious challenge. I had to first do the language of the spell, then put the structure of the wings over them. Then I had to go through and do each individual feather.

I started strong, getting the symbols, runes, and sigils in place in just under two hours. Then I downed my first Gatorade and started outlining the wings.

I started getting tired after the wings were outlined. That was about hour four. But I still had the detail work to do.

My arm was aching where I was stabbing the needles into his back every few seconds. But I knew I couldn't stop. I switched to my other arm, which helped, but only for a few hours.

He was whimpering still, but hadn't passed out. He did, but not until hour seven.

I was noticing my hunger around hour six, but couldn't stop to eat. Can't pause a spell while it's being cast. I can drink tea while I work, but that's never more than a few seconds pause between parts of the spell. I wish I'd thought about one of those health smoothies to cover the hunger. But I hadn't, and I couldn't just stop and make one, so I was just hungry.

By hour eight I was starving, but it looked so close to being done that I was able to keep focus.

Hour nine went slowly. Or too fast. I was too slow. Point is: I got less done during the ninth hour than I had during any of the other hours before it. I thought I had only about thirty minutes left when I came to the end of hour eight, but I had barely gotten half of that done during hour nine.

I eventually finished, and saw by the clock that it had taken just under eleven hours. I was exhausted. Jason was still passed out. My arms hurt so much that my fingers were distorted into claws. I fell asleep in a chair about thirty seconds after cleaning up Jason's back.

It worked. When he jumped out of the plane, he landed right next to where I was waiting for him, and he did it without using the parachute. I did not go up there and jump out of a plane with him, because I was only eighteen, though I was already smart enough not to jump out of a perfectly good airplane.

CHAPTER TWELVE

My second client for the day wants something occult like, but not 'real'; he wants a Batman symbol, but with Cthulhu instead of a bat. That's cute, it's clever, and it was pretty easy to draw. He gave me a reference picture (apparently it's on a T-shirt somewhere) but wanted things in more crisp, sharp angles. I had to distort things just a bit to get it to fit on his shoulder, but that's one of the easiest things ever. It's not like he wanted *actual* non-euclidean geometry or anything. I hate doing those; they fuck with my eyes.

We chat about nothing important, about how many times he's gotten ink before, about how his last one is doing—a few months ago I did an Elder Sign on his wrist. It's a binding symbol from the Cthulhu universe, and he wanted it on his wrist as a way of preventing him from committing suicide. I almost put real magic in it when he told me that.

So I asked how that was doing, how he was doing. Seems life is on a bit of an upswing for him. That's good. He's picking up more hours at work, which is why he could afford another tat, and he heard there is a contest for nerdy tattoos coming up, and wanted something fresh to enter with. All his ink is Cthulhu related, but this one crosses over into other nerd territory (nerditory?), so he thinks he has a better chance.

All I can do is my best. Lucky for him, I'm good at my job. I manage to make the bat wings look almost crystalline, sharp edges that still give the rounded look enough to make it clear what the symbol is, yellow dripping from the tentacles that go out through the bottom of the symbol, little flecks of other colors to hint that there might be something more going on. He's really happy with it.

It's kind of relaxing to do a normal tattoo. I mean, I do them all the time. Most of my work is normal. But it's nice, with all this shit going on, all these things I have to think about, to just do something fun.

Which makes client number three a bit more difficult. She wants a tattoo for the lost, the names of the people who were important in her life who died. There's her father, her sister, two best friends, and Robin Williams. She didn't know Robin, but he was important, and she wants him to be a part of it. She doesn't care what it looks like, so long as the names are all there.

I debated making a silhouette of Robin Williams with the other names inside of it, but I couldn't find an image that would be obviously him from a distance. I could've done the genie from Aladdin, but I feel like that would be too cheesy and kind of defeat the purpose.

Still, Williams was just a tornado of comedy chaos. Maybe there's something there. But it might be confused with a Tasmanian Devil or some shit.

I could go with the name Robin, with each letter made up of the other names. It's really hard to do small lettering. Well, it's not hard to do, but it's hard to keep it making sense over time. Healing tends to blur things a bit, so small lettering won't exactly make sense after a while. And to get 'Williams' hidden in a lower case 'n' isn't going to be easy.

I don't want to do a cross or a tombstone. That's way too morbid. But the hidden letters thing might work.

Eventually, I draw up a firework display with two smiley faces. One name around the outside of each circle and one that makes the smiles. For the eyes, I use the letters in her dad's name, Jack, so that each eye is a single letter. That should stay visible for a good long time.

She loves it. The only thing she asks is that we make one of the smiling faces frowning, so it's like a comedy/tragedy mask thing. She wants to make sure that there are other explanations for it, in case she doesn't want to give the whole story. So we put Robin in the frown, her best friends in the circles, her sister in the smile, and dad in the eyes. Then I use a lot of colors to make it look more like fireworks, like it's actually exploding.

That takes the full three hours, but she tips well.

"You want to go get something to drink?" That's Heather. Sweet girl. She runs the shop, in the sense that she manages things like appointments, but also in the sense that she owns the place. She's not much of an artist herself, but she loves tattoos and she *is* trained as a piercer. But you can't very well expect to run a piercing parlor. I don't think. That's why she has the rest of us on to make pretty art on skin.

I sigh. "I'm sorry, I can't. I have something I have to do." Something bad. Something dangerous. Something... violent.

She shrugs. "Maybe next time." Heather cannot be broken. She smiles with those two dimple piercings and goes on her merry way, not feeling rejected in the slightest, but actually taking me at my word. And meaning hers. She'll get me out drinking at some point.

And then she'll have too much, try to sleep with me or with anyone else, and I'll put her to bed. Alone. Again.

It's kind of a pattern.

INTERLUDE TWELVE

So I passed my exam. What next? I was a witch, an expert at symbol magic. I could have applied to be part of a coven, but I didn't bother. Jason wasn't a member of one, so I saw no point in it. Besides, I wasn't sure I was going to stay in Philadelphia.

For my eighteenth birthday, Jason gave me a set of my own wings. They weren't nearly as intricate as the ones I made for him. It was more a 'fall less hard' pair of wings than it was 'fly around.' Part of this was that I didn't have the power to handle the wings I made from him. Part of it was that I didn't want to spend ten fucking hours getting a tattoo. But most of it, honestly, was that I was afraid of heights. I wasn't looking to overcome that fear, so I didn't want to test the wings by jumping out of a plane or even off a building. I was willing to jump from the second floor, but that was about it.

Even still, my fourth magical tattoo was brutal. It wasn't ten hours, but it was five. Longer than any of my others. I didn't pass out, but it was a pretty near thing.

CHAPTER THIRTEEN

If things are happening the way I think they are, I'm going to have to get violent. There are demonic asses that will need to get kicked. So I might as well go prepared. When I get home, I trade out my comfy jeans for thick leather pants and put on an equally thick leather vest. It may look sexy, I suppose, but I think of it as armor. And the vest as an arsenal.

Not because it's leather. Because of the twelve throwing knives hidden in it. I make sure they're all silver and sanctified steel, ready and waiting to put the major hurt on some demons. I also slide a kukri into a spine sheath, letting my hair cover the handle. Kukris are great knives, practically short swords. They curve inward and they're heavy. They're actually designed for decapitation. Hopefully it won't come to that.

I once again look at the sewing machine that will work on leather and consider putting some glyphs on my armor to make it work better. But it would ruin the aesthetic, and I'm not entirely sure it would work. I can't really do it until I have a test pair that I won't mind getting destroyed. At least, that's what I keep telling myself.

I put leather arm guards on both forearms. They look like they could hold knives, but they don't. It's a gimmick; if people see empty knife sheaths, they assume that means I'm not carrying. The ones hidden in the vest are way better concealed. Another strap around my upper arms, these ones with a glyph written beneath the steel band to basically help any stray metal—like shrapnel or something—hit the steel instead of the flesh.

Once I'm all loaded for war, I head out to my first stop. The one I really hope won't need to get violent. The one demon I really hope is not involved.

Maxine.

I give her the benefit of the doubt and don't kick the door down. She smiles at me when I come in, but the smile quickly shifts from happy to nervous. Maxine is a mind reader, but I don't think she needed that to see how pissed off I am.

"AJ, what happened?" she asks.

"Did your people do this?" I ask. "Did they create a bunch of witches to start a war?"

She looks confused. "That seems like a really dumb idea," she says. "Why would you give an enemy more power just in time for a war?"

I shake my head. "They don't want to fight the witches. They want everyone *else* to." Maxine still doesn't seem to get it. That's actually a good sign. "Imagine if the demons traded magical power for souls and increased the number of witches above the Threshold by a few hundred percent. Then the witches start getting whittled down. Sometimes the ones that sold their souls, sometimes not. And then, when it's all over..."

I wave my hand to try to help her make the connection.

"They... collect the souls?" she asks.

"Leaving us with a whole lot fewer witches."

She snaps her fingers. "And *then* we go to war!" she says. "Oh, that *is* clever. Did you think of that? Can I use it?"

I nearly growl at her. "No. Maxine, I'm telling you that this is already happening, at least the first step of it. I wanted to know if you were a part of it."

"I told you, I don't do acquisitions. I'm not all that popular among the demon crowd." She shrugs. "Outside the bedroom at least." She smirks and looks me up and down. "You look so sexy in leather," she says. "And the anger rolling off you is just... delicious."

"Really not in the fucking mood, Max."

She giggles at the double entendre. It wasn't intentional. "Fine, fine," she says. "What do you want? What are you in the mood for?"

"How about a door I can kick down and a bunch of demon assholes I can beat the shit out of?"

She shrugs. "I can give you the door and the demons, but I can't promise you'll be able to kick their asses. Some of them are pretty tough."

I glare and half snarl. "I'm not worried," I say.

She nods. "Yeah. That's what I'm afraid of."

INTERLUDE THIRTEEN

Next, I got a job at a tattoo parlor. Another apprenticeship. I could draw straight lines better than anyone, and I was super good at making occult-looking things. So I already had a leg up.

My teacher, Greg, was a former military type. I don't know what branch, but I know that part of him will always be in the military. He likes to take his tattoo gun apart every day at the end of the day, cleaning each part and putting it back together in the morning. This is, overall, a bad idea. The pieces don't need to be taken apart, they are fragile and break easily, and there is more of a chance of it getting unsanitary when it is handled piece by piece than when it is handled on its own.

But it was Greg's shop, Greg's equipment, and Greg's rules. I told myself I didn't have much choice: I didn't know anyone else in Philly, so if it didn't work out, I had nowhere to go. Therefore, I had to accept whatever he told me. But the truth is that my parents would have sent me money to fly back to Chicago if I wanted to, and Jason was still around. In fact, I was technically still living with him, though he did start charging me rent once I got the job as an apprentice.

Greg taught me a lot about art. Not just the precision and

careful lines that Jason had drilled into me; he taught me about colors, shading, and drawing swooping lines. He showed me the grace that a design can have, and the beauty that less precise artwork can still have.

He didn't like the tattoo on my arms, and kept suggesting that I cover all those weird symbols up with something prettier.

There's a reason most tattoo artists have a lot of tattoos. Your own skin is a canvas you take with you everywhere, and it's always a good idea to practice when you have an idea. That's not how you learn, of course; you learn by practicing on fruit or on synthetic skin. But once you get past that stage, it's pretty common to refine your skills on yourself. And you get bored. So you try little things just to be funny. Also, according to Greg, clients are more likely to be comfortable getting ink from you if you have a lot of ink yourself. They won't feel judged that way.

So I ended up doodling on myself quite a bit with a tattoo gun. I drew whatever I was working on, whatever Greg suggested. Eventually, I decided to just do a large cover up half sleeve on both arms, so it didn't really matter what I drew in the meantime.

And a regular tattoo was almost laughable to me. Especially after my eighteenth birthday. So I gave myself a lot of little tattoos. Cartoon characters, movie monsters, eagles, flags— literally whatever Greg was teaching me, I'd put a tattoo to that effect on my arm. After a little while, it did not look good. Too cluttered, too random.

Which is when I covered up the whole arm with a solid color. I did that when Greg was teaching me about cover ups. There are some differences; mostly that cover ups have to be really dark, and often hurt more than the original tattoo. I paid attention to the differences. Mostly so I could explain the difference to other clients. I ended up with arrows at the top, then decided to have them trail into little tentacles at the end of my half sleeves. I didn't want it to *look* like a coverup.

CHAPTER FOURTEEN

She makes me let her drive; it's her condition for telling me where to go. When we get there, I take a deep breath. "Are you ready for this?" I ask.

She laughs. "Oh, I'm not coming in with you," she says. "There's going to be fighting, and I'm absolute crap at that."

"You're a demon, Max."

"A *sex* demon," she says. "Who is submissive."

I shrug. "I'm submissive."

She shakes her head. "But there's more to you than sex. Sex is pretty much all I am." She shrugs as if that doesn't bother her. "That's the deal."

"Then why did you want to drive?"

"So I can take you to a hospital or something when you come out."

"And if I don't come out?"

She shrugs again. "Been fun knowing you," she says.

Great. Real inspirational. I slam the car door a bit harder than I have to. Not quite hard enough to break or bend anything, but damned close.

It's a club. Why is it always a club? We're nowhere near the strip downtown, or the set of bars and clubs around Hennepin and University. We're not near the 331 at University and Broadway. This really is a terrible location for a club. Kind of out of the way, practically in the warehouse district. Far away from any authority figures, and far enough away to stop anyone from really being able to escape. Terrific.

There's a bouncer outside, and I don't need the tingle on my ass to tell that he's not human. A werewolf. Really? What kind of wolf agrees to bounce for demons?

"I'm gonna need to see some ID," he says, holding up a hand.

I look down at it, consider breaking it. "I'm here on official business," I say, showing him my blank card. "Have you considered taking tonight off?"

He raises an eyebrow. "So it's gonna be like that?" he asks.

I nod.

He shrugs. "I can't let someone who intends harm into the club," he says. "That's the deal."

"So just leave," I say. "It's not letting someone in."

He shakes his head. "Can't do it," he says. "I know you're intending to be violent. I can fucking smell it on you. You have to go through me to get inside." He sounds resigned, and not particularly looking forward to this.

I raise an eyebrow. "Any particular direction through you I should or shouldn't try?" I ask.

"Well, I'd rather you not kill me," he says. "But otherwise, we're going to have to throw down, whether I have a bum knee or not." He points to his right knee.

I nod and look him in the eye. Without changing my stance, my foot kicks out, turning sideways and slamming the sole of it right against his right knee, bending it in a direction it's not supposed to bend. I follow up with a right cross as he buckles.

He's not unconscious; just dazed. He's not getting up any time soon, but he at least *tried* to stop me.

And now there's a door I can kick down. It's heavy, probably too heavy for a girl my size to be able to break down even with three or four kicks.

My first one knocks it off the hinges and into someone supposedly checking ID.

This kind of entrance isn't normal in the club. It's not really normal anywhere, and all eyes are on me. Music is still playing. Stone Temple Pilots. At least they have good taste.

Most people are standing there like deer in headlights, not sure what is happening, not sure where they want to be, not sure how to get away. The bartender is already hiding. People in the back are looking mildly put out. And between me and them, half a dozen security types.

The first two are normal humans. In good shape, and from the way they stand, experienced in fighting, probably boxing. Maybe I can bluff my way past. "You guys really should just let me by," I say. "Then we won't cause a scene."

Not that knocking a steel door off its hinges was exactly subtle...

They step forward and tower over me. "Ma'am, we're going to have to ask you to leave."

I shake my head. "On my shield or not at all," I say. They don't get it. No one pays attention to history anymore.

Guy on the left reaches out to take my shoulder. I roll my arm, wrapping his up so my forearm is under his elbow, ready to bend it the wrong way. When guy on the right takes a swing, I turn my hips and toss guy on the left into the blow. From the looks of it, and the brass knuckles guy number two is wearing, I'm glad guy number one took it and not me.

I drop my grip as guy on the right comes at me again with a cross hit. I duck under it, bending at the knees so his uppercut goes through empty air. Then I slam an arm bar up between his legs hard enough to lift him off the ground.

At this point, the other security are heading towards me, and the patrons are heading towards the exit.

I check to make sure guy on the left isn't planning on getting up, pretty certain his partner isn't, by the way he curls into the fetal position and starts to cry. I get ready for the next set.

These four aren't human. That's bad. They don't have auras. That's worse. I take a step back and put my hands behind my back, sliding two of my throwing knives out of the vest.

"I'm here on official business," I tell them. "Fully sanctioned." That last bit may not be entirely true, but the threat that I can get away with burning the building down and killing everyone inside it might just stop some of the violence.

Nope.

Instead, it seems to escalate things. All four of them go for guns.

I throw a knife at the hand of the first guy to reach for steel, then one at the hand of the closest one to me. I can't throw at two different targets at once; brain doesn't work that way. But I'm pretty fast at switching, and I *can* throw with either hand. I can also dive for cover behind a table, and prop it up in the hopes that it'll stop bullets.

From the hissing sounds, at least one of my knives hit the target. From the thuds against the table, it's bullet proof. And from the resounding silence that follows, they're not just unloading on it, hoping to get lucky.

I was really hoping they'd do that. It takes a long time to reload, a lot longer than people think. I could take all four of them out while they were reloading. I don't have to reload my knives beyond just drawing them, and they're rigged to do that nice and quick. So that would have been ideal.

But no. These guys are actual pros, and they just wait. I know the guns are pointed at the table, and I can hear them starting to move around. They're going to surround me, or flank me, or whatever it's called. And I'm not immune to bullets.

I keep considering it, but the cost will probably be way too high.

"Last warning," I say, trying to put some confidence in my

voice. "Drop the guns and take the night off. Let's be civilized."

They don't answer. That's bad.

There's a chair right in front of me. Used to be set at the table I'm hiding behind. I kick it up into the air. Sure enough, it gets blasted. Three quick bursts of two. These guys are serious pros. I don't have time to look, but I'm guessing the groupings are pretty solid.

The chair lands off to the right of where it was, on its side. So the last shots came from the left, meaning that's where one of them is moving. But if he fired last, was it because he's slower than the others, because he's closer to me, or because he's farther away?

You know, if Maxine had come in with me, she could at least read their minds and help out a little. If I hadn't known she was a coward for years, I'd think she set me up.

I twirl a throwing knife in each hand, looking back and forth, trying to figure out which one is going to come first. I move just the side of my head enough to see that there's one guy aiming at me straight on, one guy on the ground clutching his wrist, and that's it. The other two are moving.

But which one first? If I knew which one would flank me first, I could be waiting for him, and I could take him down. But if I guess wrong, I'll have my back to someone with a gun who not only knows how to use it, but who has no soul to slow him down.

Fucking guns. How come Batman never has these problems?

I try kicking another chair, but they don't fall for it twice. I can kind of hear the others moving around, but it sounds like they're moving pretty well together.

"If you surrender, we promise you will survive the night," says the guy directly across the table from me.

Not the greatest promise. But it gives me a better idea of where everyone is. They wouldn't start threatening me until they were almost in position.

"What, so you'll wait until dawn to kill me?" I ask. I put my feet beneath me and get ready to spring. This is either going to work and be awesome, or hurt like hell for a few seconds before I die. I don't like those odds.

He laughs. He's stalling.

They must be close.

"We won't *kill* you." The way he emphasizes that word does not make me feel better. "If you surrender. Now."

It might be some kind of signal. Hopefully it is. I stand up and dive over the table, throwing both knives at the guy with the gun. My right hand throw hits right where I was aiming, taking off his trigger finger and making him drop the gun. The left hand throw should have been to the chest—painful and dangerous, but not exactly lethal.

I wasn't intending to hit him in the throat. Honest.

There are gunshots again, as the two others come out of their hiding spots and unload where I had been just a few seconds ago. I roll to my feet and end up next to the guy with the knife in his throat.

Good news: he's a demon, so this might not kill him. Bad news: the knives are sanctified steel and laced with silver. Which means it's gotta feel like acid, and the wound isn't going to just close up as soon as I pull the knife out.

He's glaring at me, trying not to cough up blood. One hand is twitching, wanting to grab the handle, but he knows that's going to hurt even worse. There's a burn on his palm from where he pulled the other knife out of his hand.

"Will your guys shoot you to get to me?" I ask him. I'm kind of afraid of the answer. He can't exactly call them off.

Wait. Maybe I can. "Hold on!" I yell. "This was all fun and games, but it looks like this one might be lethal. I can fix him, but not if you guys are still trying to kill me. Toss out your guns and step where I can see you, or he's going to die."

It's a gamble. Death for demons isn't quite like death for the rest of us. Some demons get deported back to hell, or whatever plane they're from, and are exiled for a while. Some of them basically just get reborn in the pit. Either way, it's inconvenient, but not permanent. They're only stuck for as long as everyone involved in their deaths is still alive. So if the other two kill me, it won't much matter if—

"Maxine DeFleur drove me here," I say. "She's part of this."

Now I hear groans, then the clatter of guns. The two guys come out, looking more annoyed than anything else.

"Fine," one of them says. "Save his life." Like it's some kind of inconvenience.

See, Max is a demon. Technically, she's as immortal as anyone else. And from what I understand, she hasn't been killed for more than five hundred years. She's *real* good at surviving. It helps being a coward. But if she was involved in the death, that means they'll be stuck in hell pretty much forever. Just killing me won't help.

"Give me a bar towel," I say. "A clean one." One of the goons tosses me a towel.

The one clutching his wrist looks at me with a grimace. "I'm next," he says. I can hear the pain in his voice.

I give him a dismissive nod and turn back to the one I hit in the throat. "Can you breathe right now?" I ask him. He glares at me like I'm stupid. "Right. One blink for yes, two blinks for no. Can you breathe?"

He blinks once.

"Do you taste blood?"

Two blinks.

Oh, this is better than I thought it would be. I didn't puncture his actual esophagus, so he should breathe just fine without the knife in there. All I did was—

All I did was sever the jugular. Awesome.

I don't warn him that this is going to hurt. I don't even warn him what I'm about to do. I just press the towel to his neck, then yank the blade out as fast as I can, covering the hole with the towel as soon as possible.

I still get blood sprayed in my face. But it could've been worse.

The towel's not going to hold for long, no matter how hard I press. I point to one of the former gunmen. "You help me get him up." Then to the other. "You get me some super glue. Now!"

They jump to obey me, and I swear I hear a chuckle from the back of the room. We pick up the guy with the severed jugular, and I have him bend his head away from the cut. My hope is it will keep the hole smaller if the skin is taut around it. I'm not entirely sure—I've only ever done this in theory.

We settle him onto a bar stool just as goon number four comes back with the glue. "Okay," I say, this time deciding to actually talk to my patient. "I'm going to glue the wound shut. After it dries, you might want to get real stitches or something. Try, um. Try not to bleed too much, okay?"

He gives me the finger, then winces as I rip the towel away and slap my hand over the wound instead. Blood spurts through my fingers, but it doesn't show up on leather anyway, so I'm fine. I squeeze out as much glue as I can right above the cut, drop the canister, and use my free hand to smear it down over the cut. I get sprayed in the face again for my efforts, but from the looks of it, he's not hemorrhaging blood anymore. Just in case, I put another towel to his neck. "You can hold this one. And you should be fine to talk."

"Go fuck yourself," he says.

"See?" I wipe my hands on a third bar towel, using it to wipe his blood from my face and from my vest. I'm going to need a very long shower after this. I know there's demon blood in my hair, I just know it. "Fine."

I turn to find the other demon holding out his hand, the one that has a blade sticking through it. I hit him when he tried to draw his gun. After what just happened, he seems like a bit of a baby. But the knife does go all the way through his palm.

I grab his wrist, grab the knife, and pull it out with a sickening squelch. He screeches, then takes another towel (they've got to be running out at this point) and wraps it around his hand.

I wipe off my knives and collect the others. One from the floor, one from the wall. I apparently missed by quite a margin with my second shot. So I'm not as good with my left hand. I think I made up for it with the throat shot though. Even if that *was* an accident. They don't have to know that.

I slip the four knives back into my vest and look at the security guys. They're glaring at me, but don't seem inclined to actually rip me apart just now. Maybe it's because I tried to save one of them. Maybe it's because their bosses are coming out from the back.

The first one to come out is giving me a fucking slow clap. He's wearing a nice suit, but you'd never mistake him for human. Horns come out of his forehead and curl back like slicked back hair, his eyes are black all the way through, and his skin is at least a little bit red—hard to tell in this lighting. He's also about eight feet tall. And his fingers end in these wicked hooked claws.

He's in his demon form, or most of it anyway. That means he's probably ready for a fight. But he doesn't seem like he's going to jump me. Instead, he's clapping and making me think of Emperor Palpatine laughing at Luke after he cuts off Vader's hand.

"Very impressive," he says. "Very, very impressive. I like a woman who can hold her own in a fight. Hold her own and then some."

"You forgot my quick medical attention," I say, totally deadpan.

He chuckles. "Quite right, quite right indeed. And no need for humility. I detest people who don't take credit for their abilities; one who is dishonest about himself must be himself dishonest, after all."

"Yeah." I stretch the word out, having no real idea what I

should be saying at this point. Is there about to be a fight or not? I've still got adrenaline pumping, and there's still more demons with unkicked asses. "Who are you?"

"Such deplorable manners on my part!" he says, sounding honestly offended. "Terribly sorry, how rude of me. I go by the name Casper Gutman."

That explains the way he's talking. It even sounds like Sydney Greenstreet.

"You can call me AJ," I tell him. Never give a demon your name. Tell them what they can call you, and they don't get the same power. Not that initials give much power anyway.

"And I am told, Miss AJ, that you are here in an official capacity?"

"More or less," I tell him.

"Ah, very good. Evasive answers to cover you no matter what I might say next. Lovely."

I flash him a smile and try to pick out the people behind him. If he's not going to jump me, I think they probably will.

"I must ask, of course, why? Exactly why are you here on somewhat official business?"

"I need to ask a few questions."

"And you felt the need to do so violently?"

I shrug. "I hate red tape. It was the best way to get your attention."

He chuckles again, genuinely amused. "Quite right, my dear. Direct and forthcoming. I daresay, you are the kind of woman I admire. No beating around the bush when you can beat it directly, eh?"

This impression is getting old. "Look, Gutman, how about you just answer me a few questions, and then you can go back to hunting for your bird, okay?"

This time, he actually laughs. "And educated as well!" he says. "My stars, but you're a rarity these days, my dear. Yes, let us not belabor the point, but rather out with it, indeed. Ask your questions."

"And you'll answer them?" He nods. "For free?"

"The entertainment of your show is payment enough for me, I dare say. However, should the questions be particularly difficult, I may ask for further recompense, but we can discuss that at a future date, should such a date come to pass."

I roll my eyes. "Fine. Are you one of the demon management?"

"Yes," he says. "And thank you for not referring to me as an overlord. Such titles were quaint once, but now seem so terribly dated, if I may say so."

"Do your people traffic in souls?"

"Such is our business, and business, they say, is above all laws." No idea who says *that*. Probably demons. "But we provide equitable values, I assure you, and market rates. And other methods of exchange, should that commodity be too valuable to part with."

"What do you mean?"

"Take the bouncer outside, my dear. He is bound by an oath that forms a lien on his soul. So long as he follows his oath, he receives his payment, and no one need lose anything."

That explains why he made me go through him.

"Okay, sure, whatever. Can your people give witch-like power above the normal Threshold as part of these deals?"

His eyes sparkle a little. "My dear, but you're a sharp one! I know you're not asking for yourself, I can see you have no difficulty in that department. But the trend, you have seen the trend same as I."

"Can you or can't you?"

"We can, indeed. And sometimes we do. Not often though, not often by a long shot. It tends to be bad for business."

"Why is that?"

"Either we run into trouble with what passes for the law," he gestures at me, "or they take that power and use it to bind another of us to get more than they bargained for, oft times in more ways than one." The last four words he says crisply, with a hint of threat in them.

"So you are not behind the sudden increase?"

He shakes his head. "Nothing so large, my dear. Though I must say, I am interested in what would drive you to that particular conclusion. Why us? Why not, say, the witches themselves? Or do you not truck amongst your own kind?"

Does *everyone* know I'm not in a coven? "A kid sold his soul for necromantic power recently," I tell him. "I don't know if the guy he sold it to works for you or not, but somehow I think that's tied to all the shit that's going down. It wasn't the only soul he'd purchased this month, and that makes me think you guys could be dealing this out a whole lot more. Necromancy that powerful pings above the Threshold."

"And what good would it do us to have more necromancers?" he asks. His affectation seems to be slipping. That must mean I'm getting close to the truth.

It clicks in my head, like the hammer of a pistol. I fire it at him. "Because necromancers traffic in the dead, not the demonic. Someone with necromantic power won't try to snag one of you and get his soul back."

He shrugs. "But he could. Magic is magic is magic, after all."

"That would make sense for someone who *trained* to be a necromancer. They'd have to learn all about that kind of thing. But if someone just—" I snap my fingers—"had the power, they'd only be able to do what they could think of doing. It would never occur to them that they could go beyond their normal sphere of power."

"It might at that. One cannot predict the human mind."

"Maybe not. But it's a pretty unlikely thing. A low risk venture, if you will. Good for business."

He chuckles again. "My word, you are astute. And outspoken. Excellent. I detest a woman who keeps things to herself. Shows her to be untrustworthy, and makes one wonder what plans she has that she is not revealing."

I need to get out of this conversation before I turn into Peter Lorre.

"Have your people been trading away necromantic power on a large scale?"

"Not a large scale, no," he says. "In fact, madam, since you have entertained me so thoroughly, I will give you a piece of your puzzle, one that should clarify things by, say, eleven and seven sixteenths percent." If my eyes rolled any harder, they'd fall out of my skull.

"What's the piece?" I ask.

He leans in, as if to whisper, though we both know everyone he wants to will hear us. "The numbers are wrong," he says. "There isn't an increase."

Well, that's just not true. "We can detect—"

He winks and taps his nose. "Exactly," he says. "And yet what I said remains true." He stands back up and straightens his suit. "Now then, I believe our business is concluded. If you would be so kind as to exit the premises, it would be greatly appreciated. And tell Miss DeFleur that we shan't forget her involvement."

"She didn't do anything," I tell him. "She just didn't want me to get killed."

He nods. "And it is her fault, rather directly, that you were not killed. That we were able to have this conversation. Tell her that she will be..." He waves his hand as if looking for the word. "Compensated." He smiles, then gives me a finger wave. "Ta ta now."

Maxine doesn't seem all that upset, or all that surprised, when I tell her. "See?" she says, "there are perks to having a demon friend. Companion. Lover. Whatever."

I roll my eyes. "Can I trust what he said?"

She shrugs. "Other than the eleven and seven sixteenths percent bullshit, probably. Why? What does it mean?"

"That the detection is wrong somehow. That the demons aren't behind this." I put my hands to my temples and rub at the stress headache already starting to form. "Why couldn't I just kick some ass and have that solve my problems?"

"Is that something you want?" Max asks. "I have some friends at a local dungeon. It pays well, and there's certainly a market for—"

I hold up my hand to stop her talking. "No."

She shrugs and turns her attention back to the road. "At least I'm off the hook," she says. "You don't think it was my people, so you don't think it was me. Right?"

I chuckle. "No offense, Max, but I didn't think it was you to begin with. This kind of thing isn't really your style."

It's a very delicate way to call her stupid, but I think she gets it. And I think she appreciates that I was delicate about it. At least, I hope so.

"Yeah. I'm not really known for being subtle or round about. I don't come in from behind. Others do, but I'm more the type to have someone else come in from behind."

Everything. With her, everything is a sexual double entendre. But she makes me laugh. Which I'm sure she'd say is somehow like an orgasm.

"So who else has the mojo to pull that off?"

"Depends," she says. "What are they pulling off?"

That's actually a good question. "If the demons aren't increasing the number of Threshold witches, and the numbers aren't actually increasing at all, then someone is faking the sensory abilities of the census takers. Someone is fucking with perceptions rather than reality."

She nods. "It's way easier to do it that way," she says. "A push up bra is *so* much cheaper than plastic surgery. And the effect is often the same. At least, from a distance."

That stress headache is getting worse. It's been two days already—two very long days. I have only one day left before everything gets out and the shit hits the fan. "Take me home," I say.

She gives me a smirk. "Your place or mine?" she asks.

"Mine." I give her a half glare. "Need bed." She winks at me. "For sleep." An eyebrow wriggle. "Alone."

She sighs, pretending like she's disappointed. But she takes me back to my place anyway.

"Who can fuck with perceptions on that kind of scale?" I ask her as she pulls up.

"David Copperfield? I heard he made the Statue of Liberty disappear."

I roll my eyes. "Thanks Max, you're a great help."

She smiles. "If the world doesn't end tomorrow, you wanna go clubbing this weekend?"

I chuckle. "Sure."

If the world doesn't end.

INTERLUDE FOURTEEN

Outside of work, I started taking martial arts. Krav Maga, to be specific. I wanted something that allowed me to do a lot of damage very quickly. I will never be tall. Five foot five is the best I'm ever going to get without a whole lot of surgery. And I'm not sure that's doable even then. Even with the strength tattoos on my arms, now covered by solid black arrows, I needed to have something that will make up for the lack of height.

Fighting relies a lot on the actual height of the person fighting. Mostly, it's a question of reach. If I can hit you twice as hard as you hit me, but you can punch me five inches sooner than I can punch you, I'm probably going to lose. There are ways to make up for that problem, but all things being equal, size really *does* matter.

Besides, it was great exercise, made me feel more confident, and was something to do.

CHAPTER FIFTEEN

I can't sleep. That's not unusual for me. It's not really all that late, and while I may be physically pretty tired, my brain isn't cooperating. There's something more going on, something that I'm missing. There's that puzzle that Gutman described, and I can't see the whole picture. It's frustrating as hell.

Initially, things looked pretty simple. Demons buy souls and give out magic. Witches get too numerous, and a Culling starts. Demons go to war with remaining witches. Big day for demons. But if they're not the ones behind it, who is?

And what, if anything, do the demons have to do with it?

I mean, it may be nothing. Maybe that's just a total red herring. Maybe it's coincidence that I ran into the necromancer kid right before finding out this problem. Maybe Michelle is just an unfortunate—

Michelle!

I don't know why, but something tells me the answer lies with her. Her and her girlfriend. I need to go to her school and get that sorted, first thing in the morning. Because if she *is* involved, that means there is some kind of spell gone wrong involved. Or maybe that it's all a necromancy thing. And if she's not, then that means—well, it doesn't mean shit, but at least I won't be haunted by a teenage girl anymore.

I've been neglecting her. I don't know if she's pissed or not; I can't hear her, and I can only see her when my septagram is uncovered. But she's patient. The dead are always patient. It's the one thing they all have in common.

So I'll go to her school and we'll look through the yearbooks. Tomorrow. In the morning. First thing in the morning.

"First Thing" is a relative term for me. By the time I roll out of bed and head to her school, the school day is nearly over. People are finished eating lunch, and those 'afternoon' classes are starting.

I remember high school. Like everyone else, I hated it. But I think I had more reason to than most. It wasn't the name; I'd been made fun of for my name most of my life. "Ash Grey" ha ha and fuck you, Mom and Dad. By high school, it was a whole different version of hell.

Lots of people get picked on. Lots of people get made fun of. Lots of people get ostracized. And god help you if you transfer schools. Then everyone whispers about why you had to transfer, about what kind of a freak you might be. Not to your face, but behind hands and furtive looks your way and giggles that make it very clear what the topic of conversation is, and that you're not invited to join it.

My freshman year was fine. People were stupid about the name, but there weren't really any problems. I had only just started developing—I guess I'm a late bloomer—and while I got made fun of by other girls for being flat chested or for not having a boyfriend, it wasn't really that bad. I kept my head down, I did my work, and I worked out after school. No big deal.

Sophomore year, I met him. Geoff, my first ever boyfriend. The guy who was supposed to take my virginity. He was a junior, and he had his own car. Which was enough by itself, but he was also cute, popular, and really nice. One of those guys who plays on the various sports teams but still helps the nerdy kid pick up his books when the assholes knock him down. A real sweetheart. And smart as hell, too. He'd scored a perfect ACT, and was pretty much in line to go wherever he wanted in life.

Unfortunately for him, he wanted to go towards me. Or through me. Or into me. Whatever you want to call it.

Over that summer, my body had caught up to puberty. I'd had to buy all new bras, replace a lot of my clothing, and ended up wearing things that were shorter than I realized. I didn't understand that my midriff was showing all the time, because I couldn't see it; when I look in the mirror, my arms are by my sides. But raise my shoulders even a little—like if I get nervous, or if I have to reach out for something or whatever—and skin would start to show.

Geoff loved that. He said that it was the sexiest tease he'd ever seen. And my not knowing about it just made it that much better.

Like I said, he was a sweetheart.

We dated for several months. He invited me to his prom. But we never got to go.

I wasn't going to be one of those girls who loses her virginity in the back of a shitty car on prom night.

No, I wanted to lose it beforehand. Like, a few weeks before the prom, before I'd even bought my dress.

But still in the back of a shitty car.

I don't know if I was Geoff's first. I was going to ask him, but once we got started, I got kind of distracted. He used protection, which was great, but it wasn't enough.

I'd never had an orgasm before.

And my magic had never manifested before.

Anyway, I transferred schools for my junior year. My hair had started to grow back, I had a tattoo on the back of my neck, and I had a guilty look about me. So rumors flew. Was I in some kind of gang? A cult? Had I been in prison? Were my parents on the run? Witness protection?

Thankfully, no one came up with 'Killed her boyfriend and blew up his car while they were having sex.' I don't know what I would've done if that little tidbit had come out. Probably moved.

Again.

Or just home schooled after the fire incident in the chemistry lab. You know, whatever works.

Point is, I hated high school. And pulling up to one, even if it's nothing like either of the ones I went to, gives me a nasty feeling, like I need to take a shower. Maybe it's the fear that I'll find some of the students attractive, and then remember that when I was getting my first tattoo, they were getting their diapers changed.

Whatever it is, I go in to the main office first, on the theory that it's better for them to know I'm there than to run into me randomly and wonder what the fuck I'm doing lurking around a school looking at pictures.

I wish I had a cover story. I wish this was one of those schools for the supernatural. I could bluff my way past any office if I could tell them I was here officially. I mean, I kind of am.

But no, this is a normal public school. There are a couple of non-humans here, of course, but by the tingling in my butt tattoos, it's a pretty small percentage.

So I need a cover story. If I was smart, I'd have one already set up. Like that I'm a cop getting ready to go undercover, and need to look at trends in clothing or some shit like that.

I walk up to the desk, which is nearly chest high, and look around to see if anyone's there. Hope starts to rise as I see the visitor's log, realizing I can just write my name—or someone else's name—in there and go about my day, but before I can do it, someone comes up to the front.

From the looks of him, it's a student worker. Or a very, very young teacher. Based on the way he's looking at my ink, fascinated rather than disapproving, I'm guessing student.

"Can I help you?" he asks, and I can hear his voice just begging to crack. It's adorable.

"I need to look at some of your old yearbooks," I tell him.

That seems odd. "Why?"

"It's for a project I'm working on," I say.

"Are you, like, a writer or something?"

That would've been clever. "No, I'm a tattoo artist." It comes out before I can stop myself. But wait, maybe this will work. "I have a client who wants a portrait of her daughter. She's coming in with a reference photo, but I was hoping to find her in the yearbook so I can get a jump start on it."

"On the tattoo? Without the client?"

I smile, as charming as I can. "I have to draw out the stencil so that it'll look like the right person when the ink heals," I tell him. "So there's some shading work, and some perspective stuff, that I have to do before I can put it on skin."

He nods as if that makes total sense to him. "Who are you looking for?" he asks.

Shit. Michelle never gave me a name. She can't. I mean, she can tell me, but I can't hear her. And I'm crap at reading lips.

I give the kid a charming smile and do something that makes me feel dirty inside; I lean forward a bit so he can get a peek at my cleavage. "I can't tell you that," I say. "Client confidentiality. I just need to look at a yearbook. A recent one, preferably."

Teenage boys are so easy.

"I have this year's right here," he says, pulling it out of a backpack. "Will this work?"

I push my hair away from the septagram and nod, giving him a little smile. "This is fine, yeah."

So I won't be stalking around a high school. That's good. But I do have to try and figure this out while some kid is watching me. Makes talking to a ghost a bit difficult.

Michelle stands on the other side of the counter, next to the kid. Close enough to almost touch him, not that he'd feel her. I start flipping through the pictures, starting at the freshmen, glancing up at Michelle every few seconds to see if I'm getting close.

Not freshman. Not sophomore. Not junior. Okay then.

After a little bit of searching, I find Michelle's picture. She doesn't look anything like her ghost. I mean, I can see it, but still. Her high school picture is all prim and proper, the cute little rich girl with a twinkle in her eye that tells you she's going to be someone important someday. The sweater made of angora or some other equally expensive fabric. The professional haircut, along with the professional blonde dye job, and the complete lack of anything so unseemly as a piercing.

The Michelle standing in front of me has black hair and a cut that looks like she used a pair of safety scissors to cut off her ponytail—but in a cute way. Her nose is pierced, along with her eyebrow, the snake fangs on the sides of her lips, and her ears, along with a teardrop on the right side of her face. The Michelle in the picture has at least taken those piercings out, if she didn't get them after the picture was taken. It's hard to see—honestly, it's not the greatest picture.

The kid notices that I'm lingering over the page, and he lets out a sigh. "Were you looking for Michelle?" he asks. "Makes sense that her mom would want a portrait, especially from the school photo."

"What do you mean?"

"Michelle changed. Like, a lot. Three months after that was taken, you'd never know it was her."

Piercings came after, then. I probably shouldn't pry, but I'm the curious type. "Changed how?"

"Bunch of piercings, different hair, different clothes. Different crowd, even different grades."

All signs of a major change, possibly a psychological trauma. Or maybe just of being a fucking teenager. "Her grades slipped?"

He laughs. "No," he says. "She went from being kinda smart

to throwing off every curve in every class. If she'd done it a few years earlier, she might've been valedictorian. Not that it matters now."

Okay, grades slipping suggests badness. Grades going up suggests focus. What could draw that much focus out of a kid so quickly?

"Was she religious?"

The kid shrugged. "I didn't really know her that well. I mean, her family is super Christian, but she never really struck me that way, you know? She mostly just became a kid everyone was expecting would do something horrible, then started doing awesome things instead."

"What kinds of things?"

"The grades, mostly. But she also started a campaign to get an unpopular kid voted homecoming queen, she won a state debate championship, broke up a fight, and talked someone out of killing themselves. She was a fucking hero." He looks embarrassed that he cursed in front of me. I give him the look I usually reserve for people who apologize for having a weird hair color.

"Who did she talk out of killing himself?"

"Her," the kid says, taking the book and flipping it a few pages forward. He puts it back in front of me and points at a girl who looks much more like the way Michelle dressed when she died. This girl is tall, rail thin, with pale skin and black hair, her eyes a crystal blue filled with pain. Her makeup accentuates the angles of her face, and her lips are as black as Michelle's. All she's missing is the hand stapled to her head and she'd be a textbook version of a goth.

Michelle points at the girl and jumps up and down. Apparently, we've found our match.

"That's Marcy," he tells me. "She's a freak."

I give a snort of laughter. "All the best ones are," I say.

"No, seriously," he says. "Like, she claims she can do things, make things happen. And she tried to kill herself a few years ago. Slit her wrists and everything. Then she was standing on top of the building, threatening to jump, and Michelle talked her down. They spent a lot of time together after that. Until, um—"

I nod.

"Any idea where I can find her? I kind of need to talk to her."

"She'll be out under the bleachers after school," the kid says. "She's always there, unless there's a game going on. Something about the darkness of it or whatever."

I force a chuckle. "Thanks, kid," I say.

"It's Danny," he says. "Where did you say you work again?"

"Inkspot," I tell him. "If you're over eighteen, come on by. Ask for AJ."

He holds out his hand in a much more adult movement than seems to fit his body. "I'll do that, AJ."

I shake his hand. "Thanks Danny."

INTERLUDE FIFTEEN

When I turned nineteen, I did my first magical tattoo on myself. A friend from class introduced me to bondage, and I absolutely loved it. But there is definitely a problem with bondage, in that once you're bound, you can't get out. When it's with someone you trust, that's not a problem. But I don't want to learn that I can't trust someone the hard way. So I made the key.

It's on my right wrist, and it's a skeleton key in every sense of the word. It won't let things lock around it. Sometimes, if I concentrate just right, it can even unlock things that are just nearby. It's like I just have to convince myself that the thing I want unlocked is trapping me, and it pops open.

I checked my spell with Jason before I applied it, wanting to make sure I hadn't gotten anything backwards or missed an important symbol. A key sigil, if you will. But he confirmed that it should work, and actually seemed impressed by my work.

"I have just one thing left to teach you," he said, when I came back and showed him the finished piece. "It's homunculus inking."

"What is that?"

"You're going to be able to give yourself more tattoos as time goes on. I can already feel your magic growing. I think your aura has even figured out how to better power the ones you have, so it will free up a lot of power for you to use other ways."

"More tattoos," I said. I was still pretty set on not wanting loose magic anywhere. It had only been a few years since Geoff, and I didn't want to risk it if and when I found someone else worth spending time with.

Jason nodded and gave me a smile. "All the more reason for the homunculus."

"What *is* that?"

"A homunculus is a small representation of a person, like a voodoo doll or something like that. But for our purposes, it's a place for you to cast a spell that will then be applied to your body. So you can take your wand and give that tattoo to the homunculus, then let the wand itself give the same tattoo to your body. It's a great way to be sure the spell works before you apply it."

"What's the catch?"

"It's way more painful," he says. "You get all the sensations pretty much at the same time. So take an hour of inking and cram all that pain into one minute, and you'll get the idea."

I thought he was exaggerating.

He was not.

The first time I did the homunculus tattoo, it was a small one, thankfully; just an alchemy symbol behind my right ear, meant to protect me from poison. It was something I could test relatively easily. Not all poison kills you. If I did it wrong, the worst I'd have is a really nasty day or two.

I did not think it through.

I figured out the design, infused the image with all the right magic, and did the homunculus thing like Jason taught me. The pain hit me like someone had driven a railroad spike into my skull. My eyes crossed, the breath blasted out of my body, and my vision blackened at the edges. It took me almost a minute of coughing to get the breath back into my lungs, even longer before I was breathing normally.

The spell worked, of course. I tried it with something that would make me sick. I felt a little queasy, but that was all. What I did not expect, though, was that my body basically just expelled the poison if it couldn't metabolize it. That first bit of poison was weak enough that my body could handle it. But when I tried something a little stronger, something that should have paralyzed me and had me coughing up blood, I vomited it back up a few minutes after swallowing it. Kinda dumb of me to try that in the first place.

CHAPTER SIXTEEN

When I leave the school, I see another symbol like I saw by the kid who grabbed Michelle the first time. It's not quite the same, but it's pretty similar. Still location, gathering, reaping, and death. But it looks more rudimentary, simpler somehow. And it's old; not a trace of magic still in it. You could reignite it if you wanted to, provided the spray painted symbols are still complete. I don't know why it sticks out to me; it's similar to the other symbol, but seems to lack a lot of sophistication. Like it was done hastily. The one I saw before looked like whoever had set it had taken their time. That would make the spell more effective; I wonder why the creator of this one was in such a rush?

I smoke a cigarette while I wait for school to let out. I'm already under the bleachers; hopefully that won't scare Marcy off. But it's cooler here, and this seems like as good a place as any to try to figure shit out.

So the pictures in the yearbook get taken in the fall, and the books come out in the late spring. So there's maybe six months of difference between the two times. Michelle makes a pretty huge public change in those six months, starts hanging out with Marcy, and falls in love. She focuses hard on school, getting better grades and becoming a model citizen.

Why? Is it so her parents can't yell at her for the change? Is it so she can prove she's not on drugs or something? Or is it something more sinister?

There are drugs that make you smarter. In the short term, at least. Drugs that help you remember things, that make you more energetic. Maybe she was on anti-depressants. Did her parents force her on them when she changed her style?

And then there's Marcy. A freak who claims she can 'do things' and make things happen, who is so overwhelmed by something in her life that she tries to kill herself. I look out at the school. It's maybe fifty feet from the top of the school to the ground underneath. Might kill a jumper, but probably not.

On the other hand, it's just high enough for the right enchantments to kick in and slow your fall. Maybe she wasn't trying to kill herself at all that time.

I have wings inked on my back. Yet another tattoo that has become common as hell. But mine actually glide. Once I'm falling, they start to slow my fall. I could fall fifty feet and land pretty much okay. But I'd need that kind of distance for the magic to really work; it takes a second to kick in.

Was Marcy trying out a spell when Michelle 'talked her down'?

I look over at Michelle, who is pacing and nervous. "Did you actually talk her out of suicide, or was she up there for another reason?"

She looks at me and frowns. That wasn't a yes or no question. But before I can reword it, she holds up two fingers. The second one.

"A spell?"

Yes.

"And you just told everyone that she was suicidal?"

Yes.

"Why?"

A frown, and a shrug.

Maybe it had something to do with reputation. That's apparently important in high school. Maybe it was something else. "Was that so it wouldn't look strange that you were spending time with her?"

She smiles and puts a finger on her nose.

It's a surprisingly good cover for a relationship. Hiding it right out in plain view. And Marcy's history of attempts would make it all the more plausible. If they were attempts, and not other spells. Some spells use blood, and some witches do end up killing themselves accidentally when they try to cast them.

In fact...

"Michelle, I have an important question for you," I say. "And this is serious; I need you to tell me the truth. Okay?" She nods. "It's about how you died." I hate that my gut is pointing me in this direction. I'll hate it even more if I'm right. "Was your death the accidental result of a spell?"

She nods, and there's a tear in her eyes.

"Don't worry, you're not in trouble." I sigh. I hate being right sometimes. "And neither is Marcy. I promise." She looks relieved. "But I will need her to tell me what the spell was for."

She nods, not looking me in the eye. She turns and looks at the school, waiting with the patience of the dead.

A spell powered by blood is pretty powerful. Not much more direct linkage to life than blood. And when you power something with blood, and you go too far, all kinds of weird shit can happen. When you intended to use a bit of blood to power a spell, and instead you use up an entire life, that spell will, at best, be super charged. So a spell that makes you younger might make you immortal, at least temporarily. More often, though, it just goes bad. Really bad. A spell that makes you younger turns you into a fetus. Or turns everyone around you to a child. Or makes you so old that you crumple to dust.

Age is not something you should fuck with, at least not

magically. And yet, it's probably the single most common thing people want to do with magic. No one ever said people aren't stupid.

I sigh, about to ask more questions, when I see Marcy coming towards us. She's taller than I expected, easily topping six feet. But she's so skinny I'm pretty sure I outweigh her by a significant margin, even though I'm at least half a foot shorter.

She has a black cigarette in her mouth. Ah, the days when cloves were actually cloves. Now they're just poor imitations. But the goth crowd will always be the goth crowd. She stops walking and looks at me. Then she *looks* at me. I can see the difference because her pupils dilate, her eyes go glassy, and she really looks around. But whatever she sees in me is nothing, because she sees Michelle.

The two rush towards each other like there is a swell of romantic music, but then run through each other like the cruelest of romantic comedies. I sigh.

"You can't touch her, Marcy," I tell her.

"Who are you?" she asks. She takes a deep breath with the cigarette in her mouth, and I see it light up part way through. Damn, I wish I could do that.

"My name is AJ," I say. "I've been helping Michelle out. She wants me to give you something."

"Well then give it to me," she says, sounding both hurt and angry. She holds out a demanding hand, palm open. There's a cut still healing across that palm.

"I will," I tell her. "But I need to ask you about the spell the two of you were casting."

"Spell?" she asks, trying to sound like she thinks I'm crazy. "I don't know—"

I hold up a hand. "Let's skip that shit, okay? You've already looked at my aura, and you can see Michelle. Let's not insult anyone's intelligence pretending we don't know what's what. Cool?"

She rolls her eyes in the move that all girls instinctively learn the day they become a teenager. "Fine," she says. "Not like it worked anyway."

I'm starting to think it worked, and way better than either of them had intended.

"What was it supposed to do?"

"It was supposed to make people see," she says. "To make them understand. So her parents wouldn't be so blind to—to the world as it really is."

"The world of witches?" I ask.

"No." Finally, some good news; there's a lot in that world way worse than witches. "I don't give a shit if they knew about magic. I just wanted them to see Michelle. I wanted them to understand what she was, and to accept her."

Magically coming out of the closet. That's a new one. I mean, it's not; people come out of the magical closet all the time. And people come out of the closet all the time. But I've never heard of anyone using magic to come out.

"And it killed Michelle casting this spell?"

She nods, her makeup smearing with tears. "It was an accident," she said.

I smile and take the cross off. "I know it was," I say. "And she knows it was too. She isn't angry. She doesn't blame you. She wants you to have this." I hold it out to her.

She takes it and cradles it like it's a baby. "She—" Marcy turns and unfocuses her eyes again. "You're not mad at me?"

Michelle shakes her head and reaches forward as if to touch the girl.

"I think she wants you to have it so that you'll remember her," I say. Marcy looks like she's about to declare undying love. "And so that you'll live on for her."

Michelle nods furiously, pointing at me.

Marcy looks dejected; clearly she had other plans. But she nods, her sniffles turning to sobs. "I promise," she says. "I promise."

There's not much else I can do, and this is one of those moments best left private. So I leave them to say their goodbyes. Besides, I've got some thinking to do.

Another piece of the puzzle just fell into place.

INTERLUDE SIXTEEN

There was also the expensive side effect to my new tattoo, which I didn't discover until I went to a frat party at Temple University. There was drinking, lots of drinking. I was nineteen, and a girl, so I had no trouble getting as much as I wanted. It was my first time drinking, so I didn't know any better. I didn't realize that a normal girl my size would be able to handle two, maybe three beers. I didn't realize it was weird when I finished the tenth and still barely felt anything. I decided to keep drinking, and was able to put away about a dozen more before I threw up.

Only I didn't throw up from being drunk. I wasn't drinking the beer all that fast, and between my metabolism and the new tattoo, I don't know if I ever would have gotten drunk. But I drank one last beer and threw up a few minutes later. I didn't understand it until one of the guys started treating me like I wasn't able to say no.

I had been roofied.

I asked him if he had put something in my drink. He said, "You won't remember this tomorrow. So yeah, I did. So what?"

I pulled back and punched him. Hard. Felt his jaw break under my knuckles, felt ribs crack from the second hit. He was unconscious when I kicked him in the crotch hard enough to rupture a testicle. Then his brothers dragged me off him.

I wish I could say that they kicked him out of the fraternity. Or even that they turned and attacked me, letting me do more damage to them. But neither of those things happened. They just forced me out of the frat house.

It was my last frat party. And, hopefully, the last time that son of a bitch decided to try to drug a girl to get her into bed.

He pressed charges. Tried to sue me, claimed it was attempted murder. But that came later; he was in the hospital for about a week, and it took another month before I was actually served with the papers.

CHAPTER SEVENTEEN

I think I can go back to Foshay and tell Stewart what's going on now, if I want. I mean, I now know that the witches aren't preparing for war, and that whatever the census found, it was wrong. Technically, I'm done. But I just can't help but feel like there's something I'm missing.

I've reunited the ghost with her girlfriend, given her girlfriend the cross. The necromancer is out of commission—probably dead by now. I know the demons didn't give anyone more power, at least not on such a large scale, and I know the over-coven isn't behind any kind of war.

So why don't I feel satisfied? Why do I feel like there needs to be something else? What is that itchy feeling in the back of my skull?

Normally, when I have an itch I need scratched, I go to Maxine. She knows all the right people with all the right scratching tools. But this isn't a physical thing. This is mental. And as much as I love the girl, mental isn't exactly Max's strong point. So I need to talk to someone else. I need to go somewhere else.

Should I ask Heather to go out for drinks? I can't really talk to her about this kind of thing. It might be good just to get my mind off the problem; maybe I can figure it out myself. I don't know.

I like hanging with Heather. She's a cool chick, even if she is technically my boss. She's all smiles and happiness, great to work with, great to be around. But when she goes out, she always does the same thing. She drinks *way* too much. Then she gets handsy. And needy. And depressed. And desperate. Let her drink long enough, and she'll pretty much go home with whoever smiles at her. She isn't even the least bit picky by that point. She hates herself the next day, but there's not much that can be done about that.

Except ask friends to take her out. So when I go out with Heather, we have a great time for a few hours. Then she gets really drunk, and I have to get her back to her place and into her bed, alone. Which is never as easy as I'd like it to be. I could get in the bed with her, I suppose, and that would probably be easier. But I know Heather's not in a state of mind to really consent, and I'm not about to do something like that, especially not with a friend. I don't want her to wake up hating herself because she slept with me.

I'm not even sure if she's bi. She is when she's drinking, but when she drinks, she's kind of omnisexual, so that doesn't count. If she's straight in her normal everyday life, that's not something I want to disrupt. Even if she was consenting. Which she isn't.

So I could go out with Heather, but I'd end up babysitting. And I already feel like I'm doing plenty of that with the city as a whole.

You know, I'm half tempted just to let the Culling happen. I may not be the one tapped to do it—conflict of interest and all that—but it would serve some of them right. They think they're above the law. Everyone does. Everyone thinks that the worst that will happen is a slap on the wrist. But during a Culling, slaps on the wrist are death sentences. So these people flaunting the rules and getting away with the little indiscretions they currently get away with are going to end up dead.

A lot of dead witches.

It makes sense to have a Culling, when a population gets too big. You do it with deer. You do it with supernatural creatures. The last thing we want is to open our world up to public scrutiny. People, normal people, try really hard to believe that there isn't anything that goes bump in the night. And as long as we hide ourselves well enough that they can keep believing that, everything is kosher. But if we start getting obvious, if we start outing ourselves and our fellow monsters, the whole system is going to get fucked.

And by fucked, I mean the army will get involved. And while any vampire worth his salt can take out ten soldiers, there are a lot more of them than there are of us. And they have bombs. Big ones. The kind they can drop from a distance and just wipe out huge groups of things.

So we pretend to be hidden, they pretend to believe we don't exist, and everyone is happy. But if there were suddenly three hundred more witches in town, then that balance would tip. Hence the Culling. We'll cull until we're sure the witch numbers are low enough to stay hidden.

There will be a bunch that just move the fuck on, but most witches are pretty tightly tied to wherever they decide to live. Uprooting means a different thing among us, and it's pretty fucking complicated. So lots of dead witches. Like that bitch Amber. I bet she ends up going down in the first wave. That will be sweet.

But that won't be all. We're talking probably fifty or sixty dead witches. Fifty or sixty dead *people.* And that's just what it'll take before they do another census.

There's only supposed to be about seventy-five of us in the city. If there were an extra three hundred, the Culling would drive a bunch of them away; no reason to stay where every infraction of the law can get you killed when safety is just a car ride away. I mean, if three hundred witches just came in, then they can move away pretty easily.

But...

But what if there aren't the extra three hundred? Gutman seemed pretty sure of himself that there isn't. The witches themselves don't know anything about it. Maybe it's just an illusion.

That's what the spell suggests. I think Michelle and Marcy were trying to cast a spell to get Michelle's parents to see her for what she really is, and instead got the entire city to see everyone for what they really are.

Witches are human, after all. For the most part, anyway. We were born human, and we live like humans. We just cast magic. There might be another three hundred people in the city with the capacity to become witches. Or maybe the spell just amplified the lower level powers that were already out there and catalogued, but didn't cross the Threshold.

If I can convince people that's all that's going on, there won't be a Culling. There will be a waiting period, a time for the spell to die out, and then another census. But that's if no one has taken advantage of the situation.

If someone has, and you can bet *someone* has, then there may be a Culling anyway. If I can't prove that there aren't all these new witches, they'll call for a Culling.

And then there will be maybe twenty of us left in the city.

At which point, going to war with the witches wouldn't be all that bad of a prospect.

Fuck. Some opportunistic prick is using this spell fuck-up to frame the witches, so they can get their war on.

But who would know how to do that? Who would know it had happened? Who would know that a spell had been miscast? And who would be able to maintain it?

It would have to be someone who knew magic. But it would also have to be someone who knew that the spell cost someone their life.

It would have to be someone who knows life and death and the magic in between.

Fuck me.

It would have to be a necromancer.

INTERLUDE SEVENTEEN

Immediately after the fight, I realized that I had broken my hand on his face. Felt worth it, but meant that I wouldn't be able to work nearly as well while it healed. I did not like the feeling. So I had an idea for the next tattoo.

Technically, there were ten of them, one on each finger. But I only had to design it once. The homunculus took care of the other nine. It made my hands stronger, protected them so that I wouldn't ever break a knuckle punching something again. The idea was to be able to punch people without fear, but it ended up being powerful enough that I could shadow box with a wall, and the concrete would crack before my bones would.

It was not easy getting through the tattoo. But I had some pain killers for the broken hand, so all that happened was that I vomited from the pain and passed out a little bit. But after that, I was fine.

CHAPTER EIGHTEEN

Necromancers are a strange breed. Not just because of the obsession with death. Any teenager goes through that phase, and some people never grow out of it. The necromancers are different because they're not quite witches, they're not quite wizards, and they're not quite warlocks. They have similarities with all three, but not enough to belong, and too much to be unique. They don't even have a seat on the city council.

Which, honestly, may be why they're behind this. There are maybe a dozen necromancers in the city all together. By themselves, not a force to be reckoned with. But against a similar number of witches, or allied with those witches, they'd get a certain amount of legitimacy.

I only know one of them personally. I've met that kid, but he doesn't count. Though I should probably put in a call to see if it's too late to talk to him. It might not be.

In the meantime, I can call up Dave. He's my necromancer friend. And that's not even using the term loosely.

Dave and I went to school together as kids. We drifted apart after I killed my boyfriend and transferred to another school, but we did run into each other a few times over the years. Enough for me to know that he's a necromancer. Which kind of came as a shock; he never seemed the type. Too friendly, too happy, too normal. But I guess puberty does weird things to us all.

I have his number on speed dial on my phone. Not that we talk a lot, but if something necromancy-related happens, he's the first name on my list. Maybe he calls me and insists it wasn't him, maybe I call him just to make sure. But we talk more than once in a while. And it's no surprise to me that he picks up just as soon as I finish dialing.

"Whatever it was, I didn't do it," he says.

I smile despite myself. "Good to hear from you too, Davie."

I can almost hear him shudder. "Don't call me that," he says. "Ash."

I chuckle. "Fair enough. Listen, I need some information."

"I don't know anything," he says. "I've been a good boy."

"I'm sure you have." As much as someone who fucks with the dead can be, at least. "But that doesn't change the fact that I need to ask you some questions. Academic, not accusatory."

There's a brief pause. "Really? No sanctioned interrogation?"

I shake my head, then realize he can't see me. "Just a few questions about necromancy in general, and maybe about the community in the area. Nothing official. You can even name the time and place, but I am in kind of a rush."

"Okay," he says. "Have you eaten yet? There's a Slice of New York in uptown that serves awesome pizza."

I know the place. The pizza really is good, especially if you're one of the people in the know. "Sure, I can meet you there. When?"

"It'll take me about twenty minutes to get there," he says.

"I'll see you then," I say, and hang up.

I was a bit closer than Dave, so I grab us a table and order myself a pizza. Large, covered in toppings, enough calories to kill a horse.

And I know I'm going to put it all away in one sitting. I eat a lot. Comes with the magic; that energy has to come from somewhere. It would be worse if I was injured and needed to heal—then I'd probably get two or three pies. The good news is that I don't put on extra weight. The bad news is that food is probably the biggest bill I have. But if I ate like a normal person, I'd look anorexic. And that does not appeal.

Dave doesn't look like a necromancer. He doesn't look like a funeral director, he doesn't look goth, he doesn't even look dangerous. He dresses more like a golfer. Partially, that's because he plays golf a lot, apparently. But the polo shirt, the khaki pants, and the gelled hair make him look more like a country club dickhead than someone who trucks in the dead. But hey, whatever works.

He orders a plain pizza when he sits. And he probably won't eat the whole thing. His magic doesn't come from inside himself. Mostly.

"So," he says, not wasting time with pleasantries. "What's the deal?"

"I think someone took advantage of a spell gone wrong and is using it to cause some havoc."

He shrugs. "Wouldn't be the first time."

"Can you guys snag a spell that goes wrong that fast?"

He shrugs again. It's one of his favorite gestures. "Depends. Do you mean someone snagged the magic and made it do something else, or just latched onto it and saw what it did? Because the second one is easy; most of us have sigils around that watch for that sort of thing. It's the nice guy way to do necromancy."

"What?"

He smiles. "Look, everyone thinks that there's a lot of sacrificing cute animals or stealing energy from the dead, but the truth is, there's a lot of energy that just kind of floats around untapped, at least for a little while. This spell you're talking about—I assume someone died?"

I nod. "Otherwise, I wouldn't be talking to you."

"Sure. Anyway, when someone dies casting a spell, there's a shitload of ambient magical energy. A fair amount of it will go into the spell itself, making it backlash, or do something weird, or whatever. But there's also a good chunk that just kind of floats in the air for a day or so. If you're quick, and you know how, you can harness that energy and get some power for other spells without anyone getting hurt. You're not stealing it, no one's soul is suffering; you're just using what's already there."

"And how does that work?"

"We set up sigils around the city, like I said." Sigils like the one at the school and the one under the bridge? "Things that will notice these spikes in energy with nothing attached to them. When one pops up, you try to snag it before someone else does. That way, you get the magic, no one gets hurt, and none of us run into people like you."

That... That actually makes sense. Find a way to do necromancy without anyone getting themselves dead in the process, and there's never going to be a red flag raised. You can get away with all kinds of shit that way. And they'd probably be indistinguishable from witches that way. They might even register above the Threshold, at least for as long as the power lasts.

Dave doesn't register, normally. His power is relatively minor. But that's the thing with necromancers. They don't need all that much to start with. Most of their power comes from other sources, so as long as they've got a little bit, they have all they need.

Michelle's death wouldn't account for that many people bumping over the Threshold, but between the spell they cast and the energy she produced, it might be getting somewhere.

"How much time do you have between the spell being cast and the magic being unusable?"

Dave doesn't want to answer that. He scratches the growth of stubble on his neck, he takes a bite of pizza, and he clears his throat. But I don't move, just staring him down until he realizes that he has to answer the question.

Finally, he sighs. "It's not long," he says. "Pretty much, you have until the next dawn. So at most twenty-four hours."

"And how quickly do these sigils warn you?"

He shrugs. "Mine aren't that great, but I can usually hear about it within an hour, give or take. I have other precautions out there to help me siphon the energy as fast as I can. I know one guy, Bradley Crippins, who just sets up his sigils and keeps re-energizing, getting a slow but steady stream of power. Others, like Carl Stevens, prefer earlier warnings. And then there's one guy who, frankly, is cheating."

"What?"

He smiles. "I don't know how he does it, or even who he is, but I've seen it happen. Energy appears, and he's already waiting there to siphon it. It's like his sigils tell him where it *will* happen. He's telling the fucking future."

"Is that possible?"

He shrugs again. See? Go-to move. "It's not supposed to be. Time is a weird thing. Supposed to be just something wizards can do, and that only because those fuckers don't believe in limitations."

"Could a wizard have made his sigils?"

He shakes his head. "No, their makeup is very specific to the craft. Even *you* would have to do some studying to be able to put them together." That sounds like the first one I saw, under the bridge. It was put together *wrong*. Because it was necromancy, and I don't know much about that. "I don't know how this guy is doing it, but it's pissing the rest of us off. Normally, it's a 'friend-ly' competition—" his air quotes make me nervous—"between us all, seeing who can get it first, whether or not you can get it all before someone else grabs some of it, that kind of thing. But lately, this asshole has been taking it all while the rest of us just sit and watch. Asshole has no respect for territory."

"Who is he?"

"I don't know. If I did, I would tell you; the rest of us would love to see him out of the picture. He's bad for business. If he keeps doing what he's doing, sooner or later people are going to go back to the old ways. And no one wants that."

Old ways. Meaning killing people. Or just taking advantage of people being killed. Like for instance—

"Okay, different question. If you knew that there were going to be a lot of magic related deaths, could you prep for it? Even if they weren't spells gone wrong?"

"Sure," he says. "Just another set of sigils around the area, and you scoop up a fair bit of power as people die. Not their souls, AJ." He's very clear on that. "Souls still go where they go. But when someone dies, their magic leaks out into the world for a little bit. So yeah, if you had something prepped, you could harvest a fair bit of that power."

"Are these sigils one time deals? Like, once they're up, they're up?"

He shakes his head. "Sadly, no. They degrade over time. Pretty quickly, actually. I have to replace mine every week. And to do what you're talking about, it would probably have to be even fresher than that. Like, you'd have to have the sigils set up within two days of those deaths, if you somehow knew they were coming. That's why duels to the death are so great."

"And if you set it up right before a major Culling?"

He lets out a low whistle. "Tell me you know something, AJ. Tell me you're slipping me some info on the DL. I know you can't do it officially. Just blink twice."

I raise an eyebrow. He's practically salivating.

"I take it that means there'd be a lot of power up for grabs."

He laughs. "In the sense that it rained a lot when Noah finished building his ark, yeah."

Fuck. This just keeps getting better and better.

"How do I find this guy with the future telling wards?"

He shrugs one more time. "If I knew that, we'd have found him already."

"I take it there's a consensus among you guys that you'd rather him out of the picture?"

"You could probably collect a bounty for it, if you really wanted to," he says. "Solidarity is great in the face of oppression, but when one asshole is taking food out of your mouths, he tends to get on the shit list pretty fucking fast. I know Carl has some scratch; he'd probably pay you for taking this asshole out."

That might be good. Bounty isn't the same as bribe, at least not on paper. "So how do I find him?"

Dave shrugs. Again. "If I knew that, we wouldn't have a problem with him."

"Well, can you tell me where his sigils are?"

"I can tell you where the old ones are, but like I said, they have to get redone pretty fast."

"Okay," I say, "where can I find some of his older marks?"

"There's one outside the church on Franklin, one at Bull's Run Coffee, one under the First Street bridge—like I said, this motherfucker goes wherever he wants."

Under the First Street bridge.

"Hey, any reason someone would take more or less time to set up one of these?"

"Sure. They usually have to go up pretty quickly. The energy of death is powerful, but fleeting. It really won't last nearly as long as, say, a spell. So when you find that kind of energy, assuming you didn't know it was coming ahead of time, you have to draw the symbols as fast as you can."

So a fast sigil on the outside of a school. Was there a shooting? Doesn't matter; whoever did that one isn't the one I'm looking for.

I want the guy who took the time to make sure it was perfect.

The one who knew my fight with the kid was coming.

"How do I find him?"

"It's like I said," Dave says, "this asshole doesn't have a territory. He doesn't respect any of the rules. He just goes ahead on to anyone's turf and takes what he wants. He's got no concern for the community, for the rules, or for anything." He sighs. "You know anyone like that?"

INTERLUDE EIGHTEEN

I still had to wait for my hand to heal. It technically healed in about a week, but Greg wouldn't let me come back to work before two months had passed, so I had time to do physical therapy. I didn't need physical therapy; one of the nice things about healing through magic is that it pretty much puts things back where they were originally. But I had two months off, with no source of income, and had to figure out what I was going to do.

I could have gone home to Chicago. But I felt like if I did that, I'd never come back. And according to Greg, my apprenticeship would be done a few weeks after I got back. At that point, I could get a license and be able to do tattoo work for a career. I know I could make close to forty thousand, more if I worked a lot and built a name for myself. If I went home, I'd probably have to start the apprenticeship over again. And I did not want to lose a year of work just because some asshole tried to drug me.

So I decided to go to college. I was just a year or so older than most freshman, and I figured it would be good for me. Higher education and all that. So I signed up for classes at the Moore College of Art and Design. I could have applied to Temple, might even have gotten in, but one bad experience had kinda spoiled it for me.

So I majored in Illustration and started my trek towards a BFA. That's Bachelor of Fine Arts. I thought the diploma would look good on the wall of my shop.

Classes were pretty easy. I'd been training in how to draw and design for a long time, and both Jason and Greg were diligent teachers. They had given me the experience that I needed to be able to succeed, or whatever the term is.

I thought maybe I'd be popular. For once, I got to go to a school where no one knew me, where they wouldn't judge my tattoos (especially when they found out that I had done some of them myself). No one would call me a freak, or remind me of my dead boyfriend.

But artists are catty bitches. It was my first experience with sorority girls. There weren't sororities, just that type of girl. The ones who lived on backhanded compliments, clever insults, and being overall very judgmental. Bitches. Yeah, that's the word. It was a bunch of bitches.

Some of them looked down on me for having tattoos. Said it was really great that I had embraced my urban roots so completely. Which is a fancy way of saying that it was good that I accepted that I was poor and always would be. Good that I knew my place.

I didn't hit that girl, but I should have.

Others thought I was some kind of wild party girl. Translation: a slut.

There were a few actual friends I made, but mostly I found myself having to deal with the whole situation of people talking about me while pretending they don't know I can hear them, or of whispers suddenly stopping when I came near. I had to deal with girls taking up fashion trends meant to make me feel like the odd girl out, to the point where they would change their styles if I adopted anything they had.

But, like I said, I had a few real friends. Melody and Autumn were good friends. We would hang out at the back of the room and make fun of the stuck-up bitches. We would party together.

Moore is an all-girls school. At least for undergrads. So most of the girls had to go to another school to find boys to sleep with. Mel and Autumn didn't need to go anywhere; they had each other. And they generally didn't mind me hanging out with them; I never felt like a third wheel.

We would get a hold of alcohol and do what every underage kid does when they get a hold of alcohol: we'd drink it all. Like, all of it. When you're underage, you drink like it might be the last opportunity you ever have to get alcohol.

Thankfully, there were a few people Mel and Autumn knew who were over twenty-one, so they could get us stuff every so often. It became a kind of game to see if anyone could get me drunk, or how much it would cost to do it. Sometimes, they would place bets. Could I down an entire bottle of Jack Daniels without throwing up? How many shots would it take before I was drunk?

It wasn't hard to tell when I was drunk. It seemed I couldn't keep it a secret; I'd basically announce it to anyone around me. I made a fair amount of money on the bets, at least with new people. Mel always wanted to take me to a bar and challenge people to a drinking contest. But I never went that far.

I did give them both some free ink. I used the money I had won through my drinking escapades and bought myself a tattoo rig of my own. I was unlicensed, but that didn't mean I wasn't any good. A lot of people get tattoos in college that they end up regretting as they get older. Mel and Autumn might have regretted the ink I gave them, but they wouldn't regret the quality of the work.

CHAPTER NINETEEN

ctually, I do know someone like that. Sort of. I know someone who has no concern for her community, for any rules, or for morality as we know it. Maybe she's the one who can best help me find this necromancer.

I stop off to look at the sigil under the bridge again. I take a few pictures with my phone, so I can have a nice reference to look at later. I don't know if I'm going to have to take it apart to understand and figure out what these ones are doing differently, or if I'll just be able to use it to track this fucker down.

First, though, my friend without respect for rules.

"AJ!" she says as I come into the shop. "With how often you're coming to see me, I have to wonder if there's something more going on." There's a glint in her eyes. "Are you here to arrest me? Maybe put me in handcuffs?" She gestures to the wall. "There are a few I haven't had a chance to try out yet."

I smile. "Sorry Maxine, not here to take you in or lay a beating down on you."

She pouts in a way that kind of makes my knees weak. "I never get to be the victim."

"That's because you see being the victim as a privilege. That kind of makes it impossible."

She smiles, one of those smiles that says she doesn't follow my logic, but she trusts that I must be right. "So if you're not here to play, what do you need? Shopping for a special someone? Restocking some supplies? Or did you just miss me and my gorgeous ass?"

Even from a distance, when she turns around and lifts up on her toes as if to reach for something overhead, it's impossible to miss that ass. And it is gorgeous. Perfect, in a way no human could ever hope to be. And I should know; I do a lot of work on mine.

"I actually needed to talk to someone with your expertise," I say. "I need to find someone."

"Dom or sub?"

"Not that kind of expertise."

Now she's confused. "I, um. I don't know if I have any other kind," she says.

"The person I'm looking for is ignoring custom, ignoring his community, and doesn't seem to be bound by any rules of decorum."

"Ahh," she says, smiling. "So you need someone with the moral imperative of a drunken slut in heat."

Always so tasteful, our Maxine. "I was thinking more soulless demon, but that works too."

She turns back towards me and leans forward at the perfect angle for my gaze to go right down the shirt that is cut just perfectly for the cleavage to seem accidental. I wonder how much time she spends making herself look like she's showing off her body by accident.

"So you basically need to look at things like you're totally selfish and unafraid of consequence," she says. "I know exactly what we should do."

"What's that?"

She reaches under the counter and pulls out what might be the largest bottle of gin I've ever laid eyes on. "Drunk magic!" she says.

Those are two words that should not go together.

I shake my head. "Magic isn't something to do lightly. Lots of bad shit can happen."

She nods. "Sure, sure." Then she pulls out what looks like a bottle of seltzer, some kind of weird blue liquid, and a martini shaker. "For most people, that's true. They can't lose control because they'll lose control of their magic."

"Yeah, that's about the size of it."

She pours the ingredients into the martini shaker and starts shaking like someone with decades of experience. Her other hand reaches down and pulls out two martini glasses, setting them down on the counter. "Your magic is already all bound up inside you. Drunk or sober, that ain't changing."

"Max," I say, eyeing what she's doing. "Why do you have a martini setup under the counter?"

She opens something I can't see and plops an ice cube into the shaker, then reaches down and puts an olive into each of our glasses. Back to shaking. "I don't understand the question," she says. "Where else would I keep it?"

"At home? At a bar, maybe?"

"But what if I get thirsty at work?" she asks with such innocence, like it never occurred to her that getting drunk at your place of business might not be the best of ideas. She really is bad with money.

Okay, maybe another tactic. "Why do you have two glasses?"

"It's rude not to offer to share," she says. "What's the big deal? Some boutiques offer champagne. I just prefer a dirty martini." She smirks. "Mostly for the name."

I sigh and gesture to the glass. She pours out a cloudy blue liquid that looks like it should be used to clean combs, but probably tastes delicious. I'm still not convinced that I should be drinking. Especially not if I'm going to do magic. "Drunk magic is a bad idea," I say.

"You only say that because you've never tried it. The thing that makes it bad doesn't apply to you."

She has a little bit of a point. "But I can still do magic without the ink. Just not very much."

"So do that drunk."

She gestures for me to take a drink. She lifts her glass and slams the whole thing down like it was a shot. I can practically hear it burning down her throat.

I raise mine to take a small sip, just to placate her. As soon as the glass hits my lips, she reaches out and pushes on the bottom of the glass, turning it up at an angle that forces me to either gulp some down or let it spill all over me. It tastes citrusy, almost fruity. Must be the blue stuff. I didn't get to taste enough of it to really tell what it was.

While I'm coughing, she refills my glass, so I have no idea how much of it I actually drank. She's already mixing another batch.

"I can't do magic drunk," I say, stepping away from the counter.

She watches me step away and waves me at the door. "Lock up, would you?" Then she slams a glass of pure gin and gestures me towards the martini.

"If I try to cast a spell while drunk, it could get way out of hand," I say.

She smirks as the idea crosses my mind. "So out of hand that the guy you're looking for might come looking for you?"

"Maybe, but I'd need to power it with—"

She shrugs. "You can use mine," she says. "It's not like it'll really kill me."

"But what if it does?"

"It won't," she says. "If it did, there'd be such a power backlash that it would kill you too. And then I'd be back to work on Monday." She pushes the glass almost to the edge of the counter. "Now come on, drink up."

I take the glass and take a deep breath. "This is a bad idea," I say, then take a nice gulp of the vile liquid. It's actually not that vile. Almost tastes like raspberries and cotton candy.

"What kind of stuff do you need to cast a spell?" she asks. She walks in back, and I hear a refrigerator open. When she comes back, there's a large bottle of vodka in her hand. Looks like it was in the freezer. She adds it to the mixer in lieu of more ice. Fantastic.

"Depends on the spell," I say.

"Well, how about a spell to catch the guy you're looking for? Or at least to find him?"

That would make it easier. If the spell works, I'll know where he is. If it doesn't, he'll know where I am. Either way, I win. While I'm considering this, Max pours more martini into my glass and twirls it around with a finger, then licks her finger clean in a way that is so erotic that it makes everything dirtier. In a good way.

"I need a map, a link to the guy, and something on a string that I can carve a glyph into." I take a long sip. It's getting easier to drink. The vodka seems to make it smoother. Is that possible?

She reaches under the counter and pulls out a map of the Twin Cities. I don't want to know why she has it, and I try to ignore all the markings on it. Don't worry about the smiley faces, AJ. Don't ask about the Xes, don't look too closely at the notes written next to some of the clubs, and certainly don't ask what it means to have three hearts and a star next to something.

I set my phone on one side of the map, hoping to hold it down, and pulling up the picture of the bridge sigil so I can focus on it. Then she grabs a package from a shelf and rips it open. Ribbon from under the counter acts as a string for the counterweight.

Which is, of course, a butt plug. A small one, but still.

"Now, you'll need a link for the guy, and something to carve your glyph with." She taps a finger against her lips. "And I need to come into it somehow. Can you use me as the link?"

"You're not a necromancer."

"But I am a wanton slut with no sense of morals," she says, smirking. She uses a pair of scissors to cut the ribbon, tying it around the base of the butt plug.

"Okay," I say, finishing my glass. Maxine fills it again. That's what, four? This seems like such a bad idea, but I can barely remember why. I should get to drawing before I get too drunk though.

The butt plug is made of metal. It would be so much easier if it were rubber; then a Sharpie would work just fine. But I think I need something etched into this. A marker isn't trustworthy on stainless steel. And I know it's steel, because it has to be able to conduct electricity.

Don't ask me how I know that.

"I need something sharp," I say. "Really sharp."

She nods, refilling my glass. "And some of my blood, right?"

I take the glass and nod.

As I'm raising it to my lips, she holds up her hand for me to see. I watch as her fingers grow to about twice their normal length, tapering into points so sharp they're barely visible, like something stretched out her fingers until they became needles. Then she closes her fist, leaving her pinky visible. She takes a deep breath.

I go to take a sip of my drink.

She picks up the scissors and cuts off her pinkie.

I choke on the drink.

She laughs, clutching her bleeding hand to her, gritting her teeth in pain. "Worth it," she says. "The look on your face."

"Max, what the fuck?"

She gestures to the fallen digit. "It's sharp enough to cut through the metal," she says. "And it's the right shape to be like a pen. Go ahead. But hurry, it'll decay soon."

"You want me to use your finger as a fucking pen?"

She nods. "It's the best option," she says. "And hurry up. I don't want to have to do that again."

Her breathing is getting a bit slower, and I can already see the lines of pain starting to fade from her face. Fucking demons.

I pick up the pinkie—still warm—and try not to vomit as I start to carve a seeking symbol into the butt plug. I add a symbol for magic, one for death, and a little transference sigil. I wipe Max's blood over the etching once I'm done, and drop the now cool piece of flesh as fast as I can.

She picks it up. "I was once with a guy who wanted to cut stuff off me and make me eat it," she says, looking at the finger and opening her mouth. I can feel the vomit starting to rise as she mimes popping it into her mouth. Then she smirks and tosses it under the counter. Hopefully into a medical waste can. "But even I have my limits," she says, smirking.

"You," I say, forcing my stomach to calm down, "are disgusting. And a bitch."

She shrugs. "Says the girl who just wrote a spell using someone else's finger."

She holds out my martini glass to me, in the hand that has four fingers. It isn't even bleeding anymore, which is good. If it was, I think I would've lost it.

"You can keep drinking and make this work, or you can puke and make it all for nothing," she says.

I don't know why that makes sense, but it does. So I take another dirty raspberry martini. How many is that? Five? Eight?

We hang the butt plug to the ribbon and hold it over the map. Often times, this is where people do an incantation. But I don't do incantations. That's something you do when a lot of power is coming from you. What you say doesn't matter, not really. It's just about focus. Focus and intent. A lot of people use Latin because it doesn't come up in everyday conversation. No one accidentally says the incantation they have assigned to a fireball when the word is in another language, especially a dead one.

I could say things in dead languages. I can write in at least five of them. But that's actually kind of the point. I write in languages, I don't speak. My incantation is what I scratched onto the metal with Max's finger. My binding object is the blood from her that I smeared on it. My focus is in the sigils.

The magic that comes from me, what little there is, just goes out in a rush. I don't have to control it or focus it. There's not enough to light a cigarette, let alone toss a fireball. But there's enough to get my enchantment started, enough to get the butt plug to start swinging on its own. That's right. I have an enchanted butt plug. In most people's worlds, that would be weird.

The little pendulum swings back and forth, circling the map. After a few seconds, the movements start becoming distinctly abnormal. Like, impossible for someone to fake. I think that's one of the biggest problems people have when they're learning to do this. They start moving the cord accidentally, subconsciously, just to make something happen. Then they get desperate for it to find something. And once they're desperate, their focus and their intent changes, and the spell does find *something*; just not what they were probably looking for.

Thankfully, I don't have to worry about that. Once it's moving erratically, I know there's no way in hell I'm controlling it. And good thing too, because I'm not entirely sure how this map works. I can't really read it, and I'm getting dangerously close to asking Max what the various marks mean.

When the butt plug makes a metallic thunk unto the map and against the table, it occurs to me that drunk may not be the best way to intercept this guy. I may need my facilities more or less intact to go up against a necromancer who can see the future.

Then again, maybe his ability to predict things would be thrown off by my next in a long series of really, really stupid decisions.

"Huh," says Max, looking at the map. "That's a coffee shop."

"What?" I look at the map, but the words aren't making sense the way they do to sober AJ.

"Bull's Run. It's a coffee shop on 34th and Lyndale. Weird that he'd be there. But at least it didn't pick up on me."

There was a sigil there. "That's really close," I say. "Right?"

She nods. "About six blocks, give or take."

Six blocks. That could be enough to sober me up. I push myself to my feet and try to walk determinedly towards the door, by which I mean I stagger in that direction and almost knock over one of the displays of various CBT devices.

"You going to be okay?" Maxine asks. "You need company?"

"I need a weapon," I say. I'd left my whole armory behind when I went to the school. A tattooed woman looking around at high school girls was one thing. Give that woman half a dozen potentially lethal weapons, and there's no way the cops don't find out about it. I still have a kukri in my car, but that's about it. Will it be enough?

I look around at my other options. Single tailed whips. Paddles with spikes on them. Something called an 'electro shank.'

I think it's gonna have to be enough.

INTERLUDE NINETEEN

I had a few rules when it came to tattooing friends. First, no magic. I didn't really need to mention that one; tattoo magic is pretty rare. But there it was. Second, no names. Getting someone's name tattooed on you is a guarantee that you're going to break up. It's just a bad idea. Third, no flash art. They had to know what they wanted and they had to approve of the design that I came up with. Fourth, no impulse ink. They had to at least sleep on it to decide if they really wanted it. I also tended not to do portraits, but that's more because I'm not terribly good at them.

I ended up giving Mel five tattoos during that first semester. Autumn got three. And there was a guy who got a phoenix tattoo from me. Another girl from school, I think her name was Raj, got an equation that she insisted was the mathematical representation of chaos theory. To me, it was a bunch of Greek. Literally; there are several Greek letters involved.

I did pretty well in my courses, but it started really stressing me out. I probably could have stuck it out, but the universe had other plans for me.

It was during that first semester, after all, that I first got attacked by a vampire.

CHAPTER TWENTY

Maxine doesn't leave her store, but she makes sure I can walk at least somewhat functionally, and makes sure I can repeat the directions back to her before she lets me go. She's helped me clip the sheath to the back of my pants, behind my long coat. I'm not going to get picked up for carrying a foot long curved knife through uptown Minneapolis. But there is the chance that I'll get stopped for being drunk. So I have to focus on walking straight. All my focus is on that straight line in front of me, and on making my boots step down one after another. I'm not thinking about anything else, not focusing on anything else. There's no other magic than the straight line down the sidewalk, the line that leads me to Lyndale. Then I turn right—RIGHT—and walk down past Thirty-First Street. Just a few more blocks and I'll be there.

I'm not entirely sure what I expect to find. Will the necromancer be there? Is it time for a final showdown, while I'm barely sober enough to walk straight? That seems like a really bad idea. Way better just to get a look at him. If I can see him, then maybe I can find some way to track him when I'm sober. Then I can fight him on my terms, which means I can kick his ass. And once his ass is well and truly kicked, I can make sure that the spell unravels fast enough to avoid a Culling, and then everything will go back to normal.

Or I could just draw my blade and see what I can do in a crowded coffee shop surrounded by mundanes who will call the cops faster than I can think. Tempting, but sounds like a bad idea.

Okay, then why did I bring a weapon in the first place? I don't want to fight, and having a weapon is usually a good way to start a fight. It tends to make people more willing to go at it, more eager to jump the gun, so to speak. But I don't want to jump the gun. Maybe I should've left it in my car.

No, if I left it in the car, then I'd definitely need it. I took it with me so that I won't need it. That makes sense, right? Have the weapon so you don't need it. Better to have and not need than need and not have. I think that's how the saying goes, anyway.

Eventually, the coffee shop comes into view. Coffee sounds like a great idea. It might help get my brain working. There was another reason I'm here though, isn't there? The necromancer? Yeah, that's it. He's in here somewhere. So I gotta keep an eye out.

I nearly throw up when I push my hair away from the septagram. I'm drunk enough to be seeing double anyway; adding in an actual double world by overlaying the magic is enough to make me see triple. Or is it quadruple? Do these things go up exponentially? I don't know, but I think I'm going to have to find some other way of detecting the necromancer than actually seeing his magic.

I stumble in the door. It looks like they're probably closing soon. I'm actually not sure why they're still open at all. Coffee shops are usually morning and afternoon things, not late night things. Something is off. Something is suspicious.

And my butt tingles.

The guy behind the counter—what's a male barista called? Is he a barrister? Isn't that a lawyer in England? Anyway, he gives me a nasty look that probably took him weeks of training to develop. It's not quite rude, but definitely suggests that I'm not cool enough to be here. He'll take my money, if he must, but he doesn't have to appreciate it. "What can I get you?" He doesn't cross his arms over his black T-shirt with the stupid v-neck, but I can see the muscles wanting to do it. I bet he's wearing skinny jeans. The nametag on his shirt says "Bradley."

Fuck. It's Bradley Crippins. Dave told me about him. He's another necromancer. And between his energy and the sigil Dave pointed out to me, it brought me here.

So much for drunk magic.

"Coffee," I say, once I'm sure I can get the word out without slurring it. I hold my hands far apart to mime the biggest cup he has. I almost tell him to leave room for sugar, but I'm pretty sure that would end up slurring. So I'll drink it black.

He frowns as he rings it up, and I see a swirl of black ink on his arm. Typical tattoo for someone who wants to look mysterious but doesn't have any original ideas. "Name?"

"AJ."

He charges me for the coffee—the kind of exorbitant pricing that marks this as an uptown coffee shop—and tells me to take a seat. He says the last bit in that very 'sit down before you fall down, drunk chick' kind of tone.

If I were sober, I'd be pissed. I'd probably smash his face in. But I'm not. So I won't.

Instead, I'll sit down at a table. Somewhere in a corner, where people won't notice me scratching my ass. Why does it tingle so much? It's one of those itches that feels right below the surface, so no matter how hard you go at it, you'll never quite get there. Like I need to carve into my skin just to get at it. And it's just the one side, too. Just the left.

But fuck me, it's itching enough for both sides.

The coffee comes after what is frankly an inexcusably long time. There are like five people in this place, including Bradley, and it seems to take forever for him to get around to bringing me the coffee. Although, my sense of time when I'm drunk has never been all that good. So for all I know, it was fast. Service with a sneer.

I need the caffeine to fight against the gin so I can look at the world with my septagram without throwing up all over these pretentious tables. How are tables pretentious? I'm not sure, but they manage somehow.

Okay, look at the other people, see if any of them scream necromancer to you. No one with a skull face tattoo. No one wearing dark robes. No one chanting over a boiling pot of something or playing with voodoo dolls or any of that shit. What does a necromancer even look like? I mean, they look like Bradley; but I already *knew* he was a necromancer. And he's not the one I'm looking for.

Did the spell work at all, or did the drunk magic just point me to the wrong place? I would say that's all it is, and dismiss it. But my ass will *not* stop tingling. There's something here, some power of death. Some *serious* power.

So there's something. I wonder if Crippins knows the other patrons. He might know who I'm looking for. Of course, he wouldn't be willing to just *tell* me. Maybe I can slap him around a bit; his face looks like it needs a good punching.

Or I could try being nice. I could try bribing him. Or at least show him my card. I need help; when I look around, I don't see anyone that screams necromancer, certainly not one with the power that will fuck with my ink this much. So. What does a necromancer look like?

That kid was a necromancer. But he looked like a kid. Granted, he got his magic the easy way, selling his soul. But there might be something to be seen there. He wore all black. He was socially awkward, or at least looked it. That makes sense for someone who spends all their time trucking with the dead. I doubt dead people are all that picky with who talks to them.

Michelle sure didn't care who I was; she was just glad someone could see her.

And Marcy is a necromancer too, isn't she? She seemed able to talk to Michelle, to actually *talk* to her, to hear her and everything. And she looked really goth too. Is there a uniform or something? She might not be a necromancer, but she sure dressed the part.

The snooty-coffee-man who calls himself Bradley instead of Brad comes around and puts a large cup in front of me. It looks like it should have soup in it, but instead it's filled with black tar caffeine. The coffee is even blacker than the guy's perfectly manicured fingernails. If he shaped that goatee of his and managed to smile a bit instead of looking at me like I'm something he'd have to scrape off his stupid black cowboy boots, he'd be decent looking. As it is, I really want to punch him in the face, and I don't know why. It's more than just him having that kind of face, too.

Maybe it's that the itch is getting worse. Or it was, until the coffee got here. Now I can feel the hot liquid burning its way down my throat.

After a few sips, there's a burn behind my ear. Why is the back of my ear burning? It hasn't hurt there since I got that alchemy symbol tattooed there. The one that protects me from being poisoned. The one that would—oh.

Son of a bitch tried to poison me. With coffee. That's, like, a double insult. I should go stab that fucker, or at least cut off his hand with a kukri. Yeah, that's what I should do.

Assuming, of course, I can still stand up. The poison isn't going to kill me, but I'm not completely immune to chemicals. If I was, then I wouldn't be drunk in the first place. I considered going that far, making it so no foreign substance could harm my body. But nicotine and alcohol both made very compelling cases for why I should just make it so they can't kill me. Though right now, I'm starting to come up with a counter argument.

I feel like shit. Not like I'm going to vomit—though I might. More like every muscle is aching, like my internal organs are going on strike, and like my eyes are considering joining them in sympathy. My vision is going dark around the edges.

Whatever this is, it works fast.

Too fast for me to stand up and cut—

INTERLUDE TWENTY

I was walking home from Mel and Autumn's place when it happened. I was still drunk when I left, so I decided to walk. It wasn't far to my place; just across campus. And I knew that I'd be sober by the time I got back. I staggered a bit for the first few steps, but it wasn't long before my magic-enhanced metabolism started working on the alcohol. It wasn't obvious that I was drunk for very long, but it was long enough.

He waited until I passed behind one of the academic buildings, where there wasn't a clear view to the street, before he pounced. And by pounced, I mean he casually walked out, smiled at me, and said, "No matter what, don't scream. In fact, you shouldn't even speak."

And my vocal cords were paralyzed. I looked a bit surprised by this, though probably less so than he was expecting. He took a casual step forward, his eyes still locked on mine.

"Don't resist me," he said.

I felt the words rolling through my mind. Repeating over and over, like a chant or a mantra. I kept hearing it time and time again, the sound practically caressing my soul. Every time I moved to pull away from him, the words repeated themselves louder, rising into a crescendo until I couldn't hear anything else.

He stepped up to me with a bit of care, but with complete control of the situation. He gently tilted my head to the side, then leaned down and took a careful bite.

There was no pain. It felt somewhat good, actually. The way any well applied bite will. And he didn't bite my neck, like in the movies. He bit down right where my neck connects with my shoulder, just above the collarbone.

It is a very weird experience, having someone suck your blood. It feels like there is a bit of a chill flowing through you, and it feels really good, but at the same time kind of wrong. But every time I tried to make him stop, the words would pound into me again.

I wanted him to stop. I knew that. I wanted to tell him no, wanted to push him away. But I couldn't make myself do it. I couldn't get the kind of control needed to free myself. I wanted it, and I felt like if I was just able to say something, he'd stop. Maybe it would be surprise. Maybe he'd apologize. But I couldn't make myself do it. I couldn't say no.

I was able to whimper a bit, but that was it.

He drank me slowly, carefully. And it required suction; he hadn't hit a major artery, so there was no spray. He was just taking the blood he needed. Everyone's got to eat. As long as he stopped in time, I would be fine. Just a bit tired, maybe woozy. But life would go on. I'd be fine.

But I still wanted him to stop. But I couldn't say anything. I couldn't resist him.

I whimpered a second time, and something occurred to me. My vocal cords weren't paralyzed. If they had been, I wouldn't have been able to whimper. Nothing would have come out. But whimpers did, because that wasn't talking. And all he told me was not to speak. Could I use that?

He said not to resist him. Resisting means to pull away, to stop him from what he's doing. So I can't do that. But there were things I *could* do. I didn't have to just passively take this. I could react. This wasn't polite society, I didn't have to worry about someone being offended by me asserting control over my own flesh and blood.

I wrapped an arm around his neck. He chuckled a little bit, probably assuming I was enjoying it. I was, but that didn't mean I had consented to it in the first place. My enjoyment didn't make it any easier. In fact, it made things harder. When I felt pleasure from the act, I had to wonder if maybe this *was* what I wanted, and the desire for him to stop is just a conditioned response. I mean, if I enjoyed it, that means that I was okay with it, right?

I didn't let myself get lost in that thought. I tightened my arm around him. Not enough to stop him from drinking; that would have been resisting. But it was enough that I was able to get a solid grip on him. A solid enough grip to break his neck.

It was hard to do, because I couldn't actually turn his head. If I did, I would be resisting. So instead I kicked his feet out from underneath him, then moved with him, holding his head in place as I pushed his body one way and moved the other. I snapped his neck from below, and he stopped drinking.

Once he wasn't drinking anymore, it wasn't resisting. I wasn't stopping him; he stopped himself. I left him every opportunity. But once the compulsion was gone, once I was able to make him stop, I was able to keep twisting.

CHAPTER TWENTY-ONE

When I wake up, I have a headache. If I were cool or a badass action chick or something, I'd pretend I was still asleep until I figured out what was going on around me. But I don't. I groan, loudly, and put one hand to my head, to try to keep my skull from changing time zones without bringing the rest of my body with it.

"It really is impressive," a voice says, not at all surprised—or sympathetic—about my hangover. "There was enough in that coffee to kill a horse, but you were only out for a few hours."

I open my eyes slowly, the light that meets them cutting into my soul and giving me a big light blur like Han Solo on Tattooine. I can't quite make them focus, and the pain is enough for me to reconsider trying. I lay back and try to roll over. That's when I notice that one of my hands is cuffed to something.

And it's the wrong hand. Figures.

"I knew you weren't dead, of course," he says. "If you had been, I'd have felt it. So you're still alive. That's good, I suppose. Tell me, does it have something to do with those spells in your skin?"

Tattoo magic isn't exactly well known. And even those who know it exists aren't all that good at doing it. It's pretty rare to find someone who can actually make the spells last. I apprenticed under one, and other than him, I've met two others in the entire country that can do it. So it's not all that surprising that this guy doesn't know about them. It's not like I advertise in some kind of occult newsletter.

Though that's not a bad idea; might get me more business. Is there an occult newsletter?

I make a noncommittal sound, and something hard and distinctly boot shaped slams into my leg, just hard enough to give me the godmother of all Charlie horses. Not much in the way of damage, but pain like a son of a bitch.

"I asked you a question. The least you could do is answer it."

"Yeah," I say. "It has to do with the spells in my skin."

"Who did them for you?" His voice takes on a tone of condescension that I thought was reserved for Ivy League admissions officers. "You don't have enough power to cast that kind of spell."

Ahh, the joys of being me. I have more magic than most, asshole. More than double the Threshold. But, like those stuck up twits in the various covens, you can't tell, because most of it is bound inside me, locked in by those very spells. I probably shouldn't tell him that.

So instead I shrug.

And he kicks me again. This time in the other leg. Asshole.

"Is it simply a matter of scribing a spell glyph against the skin and then tattooing it?" His voice is closer, and I risk opening my eyes again.

It's Coffee Asshole. I should've known. That's all I can really make out before the pain makes me close them again. What was his name? Bradley? Fuck, he was supposed to be helping me, not trying to kill me.

"Kind of," I tell him. My voice sounds like I've been gargling gravel. Kinda sexy, in a different circumstance. "Need the right materials to make it permanent."

"Hmm," he says. I hear him take a few steps. "And you're one of the council's hit people, aren't you? So it's your job to initiate a purge. Fascinating."

I don't like where this is going.

I feel his hand on my wrist, and the cuff loosens. Okay, I kinda like where this is going now. Then he lifts me up, though I can't feel where he's touching me. Magic. That's a lot of power to throw around so casually.

"For it to work best, you'd have to be purified," he says, walking a few steps ahead of me. He doesn't seem to get any further away, which means we're both moving. I hear a door open, and then I get hit with this wave of dry heat. "Which, I'm afraid, means you're going to have to sweat out some toxins." I feel something metal against my wrist—the other wrist this time—and then hear a cuff lock in place. He double locks it, which suggests this isn't his first time with handcuffs. In another circumstance, I might find that appealing.

"There are bottles of water here for when you get thirsty," Bradley says. "I suppose you could just let yourself die." There's the sound of a pen cap being removed, and then him drawing something. My eyes still don't want to work. "Which is all right, too," he says. "Though I have much better plans that will keep you alive for some time. This really doesn't have to end badly for you."

I feel warm wood under my shoulder as his spell releases me.

"You've got several hours to think about it. If we work together, we can do some amazing things."

Then I hear a door close. It's a thick door. Airtight, I think. There's no lack of air in here, it's just hot. And dry.

I open my eyes a bit, and thankfully, the light is dimmer. It's a sauna. He just locked me up in a fucking sauna.

What an asshole.

*   *   *

Asshole or not, he did have a point about needing to purify my body. And someone made a really good point about how saunas are relaxing and I should just lay there and let my muscles relax from all that poison. That one may have been me.

But I can't let myself drift off. I don't want to die, and sleeping in a sauna is, while not the easiest way to do it, one way to expire earlier than expected.

From the sigil on the door, it looks like he wasn't kidding about that being acceptable. It's the same sigil as under the bridge. Drawn in the same hand, with the same care. I guess maybe the drunk magic worked after all. And now he's set up in case I *do* die in here.

Technically, that's not illegal. It's not like he's draining my soul. He left me water, and told me that he doesn't expect or even *want* me to die. He's just prepared in case it should happen. It's passive necromancy. Nothing wrong with that.

I mean, he *did* try to just up and kill me. But that was poison, not magic. I've got no jurisdiction for that unless I can be sure he tried to poison me magically. And I don't think he did. I think that was run of the mill cyanide or something like that. And I can't exactly press charges in the mortal world. There'll be no sign of the poison in my blood, and the fact that I'm still alive and talking makes a really strong argument that he didn't successfully kill me. It would be my word against his.

And the word of a tattoo artist claiming to have been poisoned by a barista... well, I don't really know *how* that would go, but I have my doubts about it ending in my favor.

I sit up after a little while, when the tension starts to lessen. The water is within easy reach, and I chug down the first bottle. Then comes the part I knew I wouldn't like.

The vomiting.

INTERLUDE TWENTY-ONE

Anyone who tells you that breaking a neck is easy has seen too many movies. And anyone who tells you that it's possible to just rip someone's head off has no idea how much strength is involved in that. Even still, my tattoos made me three times stronger than I should have been, and the Krav Maga had put me in pretty good shape. I broke his neck one way, then the other. I turned it until it spun all the way around. I pushed down on his shoulder and pulled up on his head, spinning it back the other way. Every time he started to struggle, I broke his neck again and he went limp. He was healing impossibly fast, but not fast enough.

It felt like several minutes later when I finally tore his head free. It was a messy thing and a disgusting feeling. I felt his tendons give way, felt his muscles trying to resist. I felt the instant when he died, because it suddenly got easier.

I was breathing hard when it was done. I was covered in blood. Much of it was, technically, my own. Like when you swat a mosquito right before it takes off, and there is blood everywhere. It came from inside the bug, but before that it was inside you. Anyway, I was standing there, panting, covered in blood. I didn't hear the other person until he started to applaud, slowly.

I wiped my eyes and turned to look at him, now stone cold sober. He continued to walk towards me. He looked old. But then, anyone over thirty looked old to me at that point. He was wearing what looked like an expensive suit, and seemed like one of those high class people you see in Center City during the day.

"Are you seriously giving me a slow clap?" I asked him.

"What can I say? I am impressed."

"And who are you, slow clap?"

He took a few steps closer to me, moving carefully but also like he was trying very hard to not be threatening. I was immediately suspicious.

"My name is Fairbanks," he said. I did not believe him. "I represent an organization that exists to keep the supernatural world under wraps."

I chuckle. "Bang up job you've done so far," I told him. "Everyone already knows about the supernatural world. There are even laws about it." I knew about that because of my own experience. It wasn't considered murder because it was a magical accident. Once we could prove that it wasn't intentional, I was fine. More or less.

Fairbanks nodded his head. "They know that we exist," he said. "But they do not know much about what we do or who we are. To most people, the supernatural are 'out there,' something they don't have to worry about. And we keep it that way."

"So you're like the cops?"

"That isn't entirely wrong," Fairbanks said. "While there is legal precedent for the supernatural, the truth is that most law enforcement has no real chance to do their jobs when it comes to the supernatural. A human police officer trying to arrest a werewolf will not be successful."

That was an understatement. The werewolf would probably tear the cop apart. And handcuffs would never work on something that strong.

"What we do," Fairbanks said, "is provide a supplementary

enforcement system. We investigate and take action as needed. Sometimes, we are forced to sanction someone, or a group of someones, in order to maintain the balance. That is what we do; we maintain the balance."

"Sounds like you kill people."

He shrugged. "Sometimes, it is a regrettable necessity. But we do pay well for those eventualities."

"Sounds like a bounty hunter."

Fairbanks smiled. "Call it what you want, whatever will make you feel better. But there is often an investigative component as well. It is more than simply finding and eliminating a target. And elimination is done only in very specific circumstances."

"Like what?"

"Like when someone is too careless with their actions. Such as our friend there." He gestured to the rapidly decaying vampire body between us. Soon, it would be just dust, if he had been old enough. Vampires make easy cleanup, apparently. "You are not his first victim, just the first one to survive. Killing and leaving behind bodies is dangerous for all of us."

"Why?"

"It is partially a question of numbers. Mostly, though, it's a matter of technology. One on one, most of us can take out a human. But humanity has control over the military, and there are very few of us powerful enough to withstand a nuclear blast."

That's fair. I didn't know the numbers of the supernaturals versus normal humanity. But I was pretty sure the numbers were less overwhelming than they used to be. We were outnumbered probably ten to one, rather than the thousand to one we once had. There's been so much more supernatural power in the last sixty years or so. That's why we couldn't keep our existence a secret.

"So I guess I took care of your problem, then?" I asked.

"Indeed you did," Fairbanks said. "And as such, you are entitled to the bounty. And as a duly appointed agent, I am happy to pass it to you."

He reached into a pocket and pulled out a money clip. He began counting off bills, eventually extending three hundred dollars towards me. "It would have been larger," he said, "But you are—or were—not yet registered as a potential hunter. The remainder will be put towards your registration."

"I don't intend to hunt things down," I told him.

"No matter," he said. "If you do, you can. If you do not, then you have made three hundred dollars surviving an attack that would otherwise have ended your life. Either way, I'd say you have done very well."

CHAPTER TWENTY-TWO

I try not to throw up on the coals or anything like that, and get as much into a corner as I can. Most of it is just liquor and coffee, so it doesn't smell all that bad. Though I'm pretty sure you could bottle it and poison people with it. As soon as I'm done throwing up, I feel a million times better. Most of whatever was in that coffee came up with it—not an accident—and so there's not much left for my body and my magic to have to fight off.

I chug another bottle to keep hydrated and then look down at the cuff on my wrist. From what I can see, it's a normal cuff. Doesn't seem to be anything inscribed on it. I pull the hair away from my septagram and look at it. Just mundane cuffs.

So I pull my arm towards me, and the key tattooed on my wrist unlocks the cuff, leaving me free and clear. Well, locked in a sauna, completely unarmed, and stuck who knows where. But otherwise free and clear.

Time to do some thinking. I don't want to stay in here until Bradley the asshole gets back; that puke is going to smell really bad. I mean, it already does, but it's just going to get worse as it gets hotter and hotter. I don't know what cooked vomit smells like, and I'll be very happy to continue my life with that fact being just as true.

It's pretty hard to lock a sauna. Well, that's not true. You can jam the door from the outside. You might even be able to put on a padlock. I don't know. I've never really studied the way they're constructed. So I guess I should clarify.

It's pretty hard to lock *me* in a sauna. Even if my key won't unlock the door—which it probably won't; the tattoo is good for personal bondage, but isn't a skeleton key to the whole world. Too much temptation in that possibility, and I wasn't sure I was willing to pay whatever the cost of that spell would've been. I'm pretty sure I can break the door off its hinges, so long as it isn't magically reinforced. There's a little window, which I can break. It's probably pretty thick, but that won't stop me. Only worry is cutting myself on shards of glass. Luckily, there's a towel in here, presumably for me to wipe my sweat off with, that I can wrap around my hand if need be.

The room is small, so I can probably brace myself pretty well and just push until the door either breaks off its hinges or whatever is locking it snaps open. The tattoos on my fingers will stop my bones from breaking, so I can hit the door as hard as I need to—which, for me, is pretty fucking hard.

If he'd left that pen behind, I could make the wood rot away, and make the door just fall apart. But he didn't leave the pen. I guess I could try using a fingernail to scratch in the markings, but fingernails aren't the most precise tools in the world, and I have no idea how long it would take to get things just right.

I could try kicking the door, maybe snapping the lock off. I can kick in the door off a Hummer (I've done it), so this shouldn't be that bad.

Or, like a normal person, I could try just pushing on that lever there, the one that makes the door open, and see if the asshole even bothered to lock it.

He did not.

To be fair, I was cuffed to the wall. I shouldn't have been able to even reach the door. Still. Amateur.

I'm still shaking my head as I climb the stairs, marveling at his stupidity, when a sound brings my own into resounding focus. I don't know how everyone seems to recognize that sound. Maybe it's movies. Maybe it's some primal instinct. Maybe it's television.

But the sound of a shotgun being cocked is somehow universal, as is the immediate paralysis that seems to go through my body.

"I must say," he says to me, sitting in a chair and casually aiming a boom-stick at my chest, "I'm rather impressed. I had assumed it would take you longer to get out of there." He looks down at my wrist. "Did you pick the lock?"

I shrug. "Something like that."

"Fascinating. Now, judging by your arrest in movement, am I safe to assume that you are adverse to being shot?"

I glare at him. I don't point out that it's actually 'averse.' I'm not here to correct his grammar. "What's with the fancy talk, asshat?"

He smirks. "I'll take that as a yes. Sit down." He doesn't gesture with the shotgun, but rather with a turn of his chin. His eyes never leave me, the finger never leaves the trigger, and the barrel never leaves its position, leveled right at my chest.

I really should invest in a bullet proof jacket. Or vest. Or anything.

So I sit down across from him. "Don't suppose you'd like some coffee?" he asks.

I don't answer.

"Thought not." He puts the shotgun on the table, the barrel still facing me, his finger still on the trigger. "Can I count on you not to do anything particularly stupid?" he asks. "At this range, I won't need a glyph to collect your death energy. But I'd still rather keep you alive. I'm just asking for a chance to explain why."

Oh, please don't be that he wants me as his girlfriend. I'd sooner fellate the shotgun.

I lean back in the chair, trying to look unimpressed, and trying to angle my body just a little bit away from the shotgun. "Go ahead," I say with a sigh, trying to sound bored.

"You came to find me because the other necromancers sent you, right?"

"Sure." If that's what he wants to believe, I'm not going to change his mind with something as unimportant as the truth.

"They want to know how I'm always one step ahead of them." He smiles. "That's understandable. I'd be annoyed too. But that's not important. What is important is the sigil on the sauna door and the spells woven into your flesh."

"What?" Okay, that's a bit of a surprise.

"I know who you work for," he says. "And I know what that means your job is. And I happen to know that there is a big, nasty war coming. Lots of people going to die."

"Because you're keeping a spell going."

He smiles. "It's so much more than that. But yes, I'm keeping it going. Which, we both know, will cause a Culling."

"A lot of people are going to die."

Bradley shrugs. "Nothing I can do about that. But you're the one who's going to do most of the killing."

Not if I can help it. "Go on," I say.

"I assume that the spells in your flesh are locked there via your tattoos? I'd heard rumors that such a thing was possible, even seen one or two little examples. But you seem to have it on a much, much larger scale than most."

I nod. Most people get one magical tattoo and decide that they never, ever want another one. I understand. The pain is just as bad every time, and you never get used to it.

"I'd like to engage your services and purchase some of your skin."

Okay, that's a new one. I can't help but laugh. "What the fuck are you talking about?"

"That sigil on the door downstairs. I want you to get a tattoo similar to it."

"Why?"

"Because then a portion of the energy will come to me every time you kill someone," he says. "That's all. It won't control you in any way, nor bind you to my will, nor any of that sort of thing. All it would do is let some of the death energy channel back to me."

"Why the hell would I want to do that?"

He shrugs, his finger still on the trigger. I'm leaning back in my chair, my arms crossed. If I fall backwards at just the right time, his shot could go harmlessly over my head. And then I'd thud on the floor, be stunned for a second or two, and only have to worry about the second shot. So still not a plan.

"Think about it. For one, it would give me a vested interest in your continued wellbeing. I assume the spells would stop working if you died?"

"The ones on me would." The magic is bound in the skin, and the spell is powered by the person it's bound to. That's why I can give other people ink. And it's why I don't register on the Threshold—there's so much of my magic constantly being drained just to keep my spells active.

He smiles. I don't like his smile. I lean back a little bit more, hooking my foot around one leg of the table to keep balanced. That gives me an idea.

"So it would be to my benefit to see you still not only alive, but in fighting shape. And, if you are more of a mercenary leaning, I'll pay you. Every time you kill, if that's what it will take to buy your loyalty."

"My loyalty isn't for sale."

He shakes his head. "Everyone's loyalty is for sale. Everyone has their price. You just have to figure out what the right currency is."

"What's yours?"

"Power," he says. He shrugs. "It's not really all that complex. If someone wants me to work for them, and they can provide me more power than I could get on my own, that's what it takes. It helps if their goals allow me to continue acting in my own self-interest. You can count on selfishness more than selflessness any day of the week."

"Are you working for someone?"

He smiles. Well, I was hoping for an answer. It would certainly make sense.

"Let's talk about self-interest," he says. "You want to get out of here alive. I am offering you a way to walk out fully intact, without anything missing or wounded or broken. All I want is that sigil on your flesh. Doesn't matter where. Doesn't matter how big. Just bear my mark, and then go about and do what you normally do. Act on your own accord, and you never have to worry about me." He then sighs dramatically. "Or I can just kill you now, take what energy I can get, and move on to other possibilities."

I pretend to think about it, leaning forward a bit, resting my knee against the table. The front legs of the chair aren't on the floor, and that's important. "How about this," I say. My knee presses against my chest and I tense the muscles in my leg like a spring. "Speaking of self-interest. You stop the illusion that spell created, tell me what I need to know, and I just arrest you. You don't, and I beat the living hell out of you first."

He smiles and gestures at the shotgun. "How do you intend to that?" he asks.

Or rather, he starts to ask. As soon as he looks down at the gun, just for a second, I spring into action. I kick back from the table with my knee, pushing the chair off balance and extending my leg so that my foot kicks the underside of the table. That forces it to go up a little, and when he does fire, the only dangerous part for me is the noise. But I've seen Ministry live, so any damage to my hearing is a done deal.

But kicking, along with the momentum, lets me roll out of the chair rather than falling flat on my back. So I roll to my feet while he reaches to pump another round into his shotgun. A double barrel would have been too much to ask for.

If the table were completely vertical, I could kick it at him. Hell, even horizontal I could probably do that. But it's more wobbly, so I can't be sure that a kick would hit good and solid.

But the table does have four legs. So I can kick one of the legs, sending the table either spinning around or straight at him. Spinning would have been cooler; I could have tripped him with the legs of the table. But straight at him works too. He grunts, and I close the distance between us.

A shotgun blast at close range is no fun. Worse if it hits you. Really, any gunshot wound sucks. I assume—I've never had one before. But getting close to someone with a gun means being able to push the barrel to the side. It also means being able to grab the gun close to the butt of it, and push and twist with the hopes of catching his finger in the trigger guard, or at least wresting the weapon away from him.

It also gets us even closer together.

People who fight tend to think of fighting in three distances. There's across the room, where you can't really do much more than taunt one another; you're too far for kicking, too far for punching, too far for grappling. Then there's the middle distance, where you can kick fairly well, but punching is still kind of out of the question. That's what Tae Kwon Do people all prefer—they're all about the kicks. Then there's nearby, where you can snap out a kick if you have to and punch to your heart's content. It's also a good distance to reach out and grapple. That's what most fighters consider ideal.

But there's a fourth distance. People who know Hapkido or Krav Maga—like me—know that fourth distance. It's super close. So close that elbows and knees come into play. So close that you can hit someone with your bicep, that headbutting is a real option, and so close that you can fight extremely dirty.

Close enough that with my hands on the shotgun, I can slam one elbow into his chest, then turn my shoulders so that my shoulder smacks him across the jaw. It's not the most powerful strike, but it doesn't have to be. The point is surprise. And the kick with my insole into the small of his knee isn't about force either. That kick's about getting him off balance.

So with him off balance and surprised, I can pull and twist and get the gun out of his hands. I could turn it on him and shoot the fucker right here. He did try to poison me after all. And he's already shot at me once.

But I don't like guns. So I keep pumping the action and watching the shells fall to the floor one by one as he rolls to his own feet. His roll is nowhere near as fast or impressive as mine.

He puts a hand to his lips like a bad guy in a cheesy movie, expecting to wipe away blood and look all cool. But I didn't hit him hard enough for him to bleed, so instead he just looks like a wuss.

"What the fuck?" he asks.

I shrug. "You want to come quietly, or can I beat the shit out of you a bit?"

"I thought you wanted me to answer your questions."

Right. I did say that, didn't I?

"Who are you working for?" I ask him. I suppose it's possible that this guy is the top of the chain, but honestly, what are the odds?

"Fuck you."

I don't need superhuman strength or speed to shuffle forward and slam my forearm into the side of his face. I don't need it, but the impact is a bit more intense when I use it anyway. He staggers back a few paces, blinking away the stars. Nothing's broken though, not yet.

"You're not a seer," I say. "You can't see the future. So who are you working for?"

"No one, bitch."

I lift a foot to kick him, and he moves to block it. So I just let my knee come up, then come back down, and I slap him across the face. Hard. Humiliating.

"Who do you work for?"

"I'm not telling you shit," he says.

I stutter step forward and raise my knee again. He puts his hands up. He's learning. So I extend the kick and slam it into his stomach, blasting out his air and leaving him a coughing mess on the floor. He doesn't throw up though. Small miracles.

"I feel like I'm beating up a cripple," I say. "How about you just tell me so I can go take a shower?"

He pushes himself to his feet. Then he takes a breath and jumps forward to stab me in the heart.

He doesn't have a knife. That's good. If he'd been using a knife, then he'd have at least cut my skin. I might have gotten out of the way enough—I did see the attack coming—but there would be blood.

But he doesn't have a knife. Not a real one. He has a knife forged out of the energy of the dead. A ghost knife, if you will. Normally, that sort of thing is way more dangerous. A real knife slicing into my breast would hurt like hell, and would bleed, but probably wouldn't be long or strong enough to pierce my breastplate and puncture my heart. A ghost knife, though, it doesn't have to worry about things like physics or biology. It would be stabbing right into my spirit, and as long as it hits my heart that way, I just die. With no visible marks or explanations. Some coroner writes up that I died of a sudden heart episode, and everyone talks at my funeral about how I always seemed so healthy.

For a normal person, a ghost knife would be the end of them. But I have to deal with ghosts sometimes, so I have made ghost material solid, or at least unable to pass through my body. That's why I could touch Michelle when we first met.

And that's why a ghost knife to the heart isn't really all that dangerous. I shift a little to make the impact a bit less dead on, and so I'm hit with his fist and the magic, but not the full power of it.

Which is not to say it doesn't hurt. It's more like getting shot when you're wearing a bullet proof vest. At least, I assume. It feels like he smashed a sledgehammer into my chest, and the padding that fills in my bra is made of flesh, not of padding (which I guess makes for a crappy metaphor). I still go staggering back, and I still lose my breath, and it still hurts like a bitch. In a few hours, my whole chest is going to be one massive bruise. But I don't think anything is broken.

Staggering back does push my hair away from the septagram, though. And so I get to see him with my magical sight. He's got energy flowing into him at a regular stream, but small amounts. That must be the death energy his glyphs collect. It looks like little IV lines dripping some kind of drug into his veins. But that's not even the creepiest part.

The creepiest part is the pulsing string at the back of his neck. A string that isn't feeding in anything, and isn't taking away anything. It just sits there and pulses, moving a bit every time he does, almost as if it were flexing a long strand of muscles in a tube to make him act. Or if it were like a puppet on a string. Only a living puppet. With a living string.

My own urge to vomit isn't just from the hit to the chest.

It reminds me briefly of that thing I saw near the kid necromancer when I took him down. Are they connected? Fuck. I was really hoping Bradley here would be the top guy, the one who seems to be telling the future. But no; he's just being manipulated. Or controlled. Or whatever. But he's not the guy at the top. Is he the one fucking with Marcy and Michelle's spell?

"That," I gasp, focusing on the pain and hurriedly pushing my hair back over my tattoo, "is three times you've tried to kill me." I hold up a hand and take a deep breath. It hurts. "First there was the poison."

I hold up a second finger and stand up straight. "Then there was the shotgun." I stretch my arms out, and while it hurts, it confirms that nothing in my chest or ribs is broken or even cracked. "And now you stabbed me with a spirit knife."

"And yet you won't die, you maddening bitch."

I nod. "And yet I won't die," I agree.

He extends his hands, and I see the faint representation of a blade in one hand, an axe in the other. To anyone else, one swipe means death. To me, it'll be like being pummeled by baseball bats. Eventually, the same result. I'm not immortal.

He snarls at me, apparently past the 'clever quip' phase, and jumps at me.

I'd be more worried if he'd had one weapon than two. People think more is better, but we can't really concentrate on two weapons at once as well as we think we can. You end up using them together, and there's only so many things you can do with two weapons. It ends up being pretty limiting. I can manage multiple targets if they're in the same line of vision, but even then I miss as often as not when trying to throw with both hands.

He swipes across, like he's trying to turn his weapons into a pair of scissors and cut off my head. I take a long lunging step, which both brings me in close and lowers my head far enough for the attack to go over it. It also leaves me about eye level with his stomach.

I should really kill him.

Instead, I put my weight on my forward leg and step into it, bringing my back leg in and up so fast and so hard that not only do the weapons disappear when my knee slams his balls so hard that they probably burst, but his feet also leave the ground.

Small mercy, he's unconscious when he lands, curled up in the fetal position and groaning in pain even as he's completely out. That's going to still hurt when he gets up. And if they really *did* burst, well, there's still a chance he's going to die.

I brush my hair out of the way just in time to see that living string twitch a few times, then detach and pull away, bringing with it a pretty serious amount of power. What's left behind, aside from the thrumming of pain, is a relatively small amount of energy. This guy couldn't cross the Threshold if he wanted to. Whatever that string was, it contained most of his power. Or took the power with it when it left, wherever it went.

Just like the necromancer kid. Someone is puppeteering from a goodly distance away. Using these other people as pawns for some nefarious ends.

I really hate the sound of that.

I wonder what my boss will say about it.

INTERLUDE TWENTY-TWO

"I'm not a killer."

"The body before you suggests the contrary," Fairbanks said.

"That was self-defense."

"And, in a way, so is what we do. We are defending ourselves by taking care of those who would do us the most harm. Please consider the offer. We will provide you with a good living, quite a few resources, and a fair amount of protection from any potential reprisal." He held out his hand, and there was a business card sitting in his palm. He wasn't offering it out like some sleazy car salesman; it was just there in case I wanted to take it.

"I'll think about it," I told him, having no intention whatsoever of doing so.

He smiled, and it occurred to me that his smile was a bit too broad. More like a shark than a person. He gestured to his hand. I pulled my hair back so I could see it with magical sight, and saw that there was an enchantment on it. I looked up at him and raised an eyebrow.

"Really?" I asked. "You expect me to just pick that up, with no idea of what it will do?"

He smiled again. "It has a tracking spell," he told me. "So that when you want to contact me, I will know where you are. That is all. Nothing to be afraid of, I assure you." Then he tilted his head to the side a bit. "Besides, if I had wanted to becharm you, wouldn't I have been able to do so with the money you took so eagerly?"

He had a point. I took the card. All it had written on it was his name. I looked up to ask how I was supposed to contact him, but he was gone.

CHAPTER TWENTY-THREE

oshay Tower. This time, without the coffee. Without Chuck. And without the waiting. This time, I get straight in to see Stewart.

"Tell me what you did not put in your report," he says to me.

I wrote a report about what I've been doing, about why I arrested the dumbass necromancer. I wrote about helping Michelle move on, and I wrote about the little scuffles with the demons. But I didn't say why I was looking into all this. I was keeping it hush hush, just like Stewart asked me to.

"It isn't real," I tell him. "A spell to expose the truth about someone to specific people went awry. Started overexposing all the magic everywhere. The witches didn't even know about it. Shouldn't have lasted more than a few hours, but the necro I brought in yesterday snagged hold of it and fed into it in the hopes of starting a war or a Culling or both."

"For the sake of his own power." Stewart sounds mildly disgusted by the idea. He seems mildly disgusted by a lot of humanity, I've noticed. "Is the spell no longer being maintained?"

"He'd have to repower it. So it won't last longer than three more days."

"That is good news, at least. The spell will fade, and danger will be diverted. Why was this Bradley doing it in the first place? Was it as simple as hoping to gain power from the witches who would have been unjustly killed?"

"Maybe for something more, I don't know. I just know he's one of the ones who places sigils around and siphons off death energy. One of the more harmless necros, such as it is."

"Like your contact?"

I frown. "Yes, like Dave. But there's more."

Stewart looks at me with the patience of eternity, but it's just a look.

"The guy I brought in. Bradley. He had a—a string."

"What?"

I point to the back of my neck. That's where my first tattoo is. The one that binds my magic. The one that stops me from bursting into flames all the time. It had to be there, because that chakra point is like the core of my magic, and the—oh fuck.

"There was a string coming out of the guy's neck. In the back. At the chakra focal point. It pulsed like it was alive. When I took him down, the string detached, and took a bunch of his power with it."

Stewart seems unhappy. There's a fun understatement for you. "Did you see where the string led?"

I shake my head. "No, but it does explain something Dave said about him." Stewart waves for me to continue. "He said this guy seems to know exactly where to put the sigils *before* it becomes important. He's been hogging the energy, almost like he knows the future."

Stewart shakes his head. "Necromancers are not precognizant."

I nod. "Which means someone else, someone who is, must have been working with him. Or using him like a puppet."

Stewart looks grim. "And you are quite sure it was not the demons?"

"They said they had nothing to do with this. I assume if they were controlling the mastermind, that would qualify as having 'something' to do with it."

"So there is another player." He sighs. "I will look into it. I imagine this is not the last we will hear of him or her or them or it."

"So what, we just keep an eye out?"

He nods. "This sounds like the sort of thing that one who plans ahead does. If this one is precognizant, we cannot hope to catch them so quickly. We must wait and react, rather than act. I do not like it any more than you do, Ashley."

"AJ," I correct him.

He ignores me. As usual. "Well done, in any case. You have more than done what I asked you to do. I am very appreciative."

"Financially?" I ask. Bonuses are great for wasting on things like credit card bills.

He smiles. "Unfortunately, no. I do not have the finances at my disposal to reward you so directly. But I have made a call on your behalf, so there will hopefully be at least something good coming out of this."

I really, *really* don't like the sound of that.

INTERLUDE TWENTY-THREE

I considered the offer for a while. The three hundred dollars made a real difference in my life. Art school is not cheap, and neither are the supplies I needed to keep up. If I was really honest with myself, I knew that I couldn't afford to remain a student for very long. But maybe, if I was okay with hunting down other supernatural things, I'd be able to stay a bit longer. It was just a question of whether or not I was willing to become a killer.

It was actually Autumn that helped make the decision for me, though a bit indirectly. She set me up with Vanessa, which changed things for me dramatically.

I hadn't dated anyone since Geoff. Too many bad memories. I was afraid of sex, if I was being honest with myself, and guys didn't like to date girls who were afraid of sex. Especially not at that age. I'd never really given any thought to spending time with another girl, but the idea ended up appealing to me. I mean, if it turned out I was straight, then I'd at least have someone I could hang out with and make a new friend. If I wasn't, then I would have a girlfriend. I'd have all the fun of dating without any of the pressure that comes from men. And I could make sure that I wasn't the one orgasmically exploding all over the place.

That was appealing, too.

Which is not to say that Vanessa and I started off with dating. We started off just kind of hanging out. Vanessa was deaf, so it was hard for her to make friends. Not many people were willing to put up with what she called her 'accent,' which was really just what it sounds like when deaf people talk. It has to do with not being able to hear their own voices. She could read lips, which made things pretty good, so long as you weren't hanging out in the dark.

But she was funny, and clever. And, I realized as a bit of time went by, she was cute. Really cute. She had this great cherub face, which she hated (she said she thought she had a fat face), with a defined chin and eyes so big she almost looked like an anime character. She was also creative as hell, already drawing her own graphic novel, which she often worked on in class. Her lines were crisp and precise, her hands amazingly dexterous. She claimed it had to do with learning to sign. And she offered to teach me. In exchange for a tattoo.

She started teaching me some basic sign, speaking out what she was signing and helping me fix what I signed back. It wasn't long before we were having conversations in two languages at once. I gave her a nice tattoo; it was a pair of hands (which are incredibly hard to do) making the ASL sign for "slut" on her lower back. A tramp stamp that only people who sign would think is funny. Just in case, I used very minimalist lines and shading, in case she wanted to get it covered up some day.

CHAPTER TWENTY-FOUR

I*'m glad you're drunk.* Strange thing for a voice to say. Even when that voice isn't mine. Even when I'm asleep. Wait. I'm asleep?

You are. Your mental defenses are quite powerful, Neophyte Grey. Without your inebriation, I doubt even I would be able to get in. It is fortuitous, I would say.

Who are you?

I believe you know that, the voice says. *And when you do, I'm sure you will manifest me visually, Neophyte Grey.*

He keeps calling me that. Wait a minute.

Suddenly, I'm back where I met the over-coven. Only most of the room is empty. There's just me and the guy I talked to. The guy I wanted to give the finger to. The one in charge. The guy in charge. Bloody hell.

He smiles at me from his seat, then looks down at himself. "Really?" he asks. "This is how you see me? I don't believe my real suit is this well-tailored."

I shrug. "It's a dream. Enjoy it."

"Fair enough, fair enough. As I was saying, your mental defenses are very powerful."

"Most of my defenses are very powerful," I say. "That's why

I'm still alive."

He nods and gets out of the chair, stepping forward to a table that didn't used to be there, taking a seat at one chair, and offering me the other with the wave of his hand. "There's no need to stand on formality, Neophyte Grey."

"Then stop calling me that," I say, slipping into the chair across from him. I don't like the one he made, so I make it softer and more comfortable. It's my fucking dream. I do what I want.

"What should I call you?"

"How about AJ?"

He smiles. It's not a bad smile. "I will call you AJ, but only if you call me Kenzel." He raises an eyebrow at me. Maybe he's expecting me to make fun of his name. But of all the people in the world, I am the last one to make fun of someone else's name. Usually.

"Okay, Kenzel. So you established that my defenses are strong, and that you can get past them, at least when I get drunk. Is there another purpose to this visit? I'm willing to bet I was having a dream with a whole lot more leather involved, and not just the chairs."

He doesn't seem phased by my comment. Maybe he's into that sort of thing.

"There is a purpose," he assures me. "I wanted to talk to you about your coven status."

"I don't *have* a coven status. That's why you call me a Neophyte, even though we both know it's bullshit."

He nods. "It certainly is. Now that I'm inside your wards, I can feel how strong you really are. You should more than be in a coven, AJ. You should probably have one of your own."

"But I don't pass the Threshold test."

He waves me away. "An outdated system to say the least. The flaws of which, I must say, you have done an admirable job both exposing and exemplifying."

"Okay, that's gonna need some explanation."

"The spell that the two young girls cast, the one that would make the girl's parents see her for what she really is. It exposed a huge number of minor talents in the area. Minor talents that may someday cross the Threshold, or may forever toil on in obscurity." He takes a breath and gives me a dazzling smile. "Or possibly who, like you, have their magic hidden somehow."

"There's no one else like me in the city." Tattoo magic isn't exactly popular, mostly because of the costs. Those of us who really practice it are a relatively tight knit group. The four of us stay in touch, usually over email. Sometimes we meet up at tattoo conventions.

"Perhaps not," he says. "But there could be. And there could be those with minor talents that have the potential for growth, that could eventually be worthy members of covens. Hundreds of them, in fact.

"That's a surprise to us. We thought that the gift was far more rare. That most of the time, when someone with minor talent finally did cross the Threshold, we could get a hold of them and get them into the system in rather short order. We thought we missed maybe one in ten." He takes a deep breath, though he doesn't need to—he's not really here. "Now, from that spell, it seems like we were closer to *catching* one in ten. Meaning most of those who could be nudged past the line never make it because they don't know their own potential."

"Or have their potential hidden somehow."

He nods. "Either way, the community misses out. And to have someone like you, someone who should be in the system but for whom the system seems closed, that also opened a lot of eyes."

"What do you mean? Are you guys changing the entry requirements?" I don't really care. I mean, it could be nice to get into a coven, but if they don't want me, then fuck them. I don't care. I can live without it. I've made it this far.

He looks a little bit embarrassed. "That we—or at least *I*— cannot do. It will change in time, I'm sure, but there needs to be an adjustment period. Politics and all that."

Fucking sororities.

"However, that is for full covens. There are no rules for under covens."

"What's an under coven? I've never heard of that before."

"No one has," he says with a satisfied smile. "That's what makes them so unique. Under covens existed a long time ago, as sort of a training program. They were filled with people who usually never moved onwards. Partially they were made to keep an eye on minor talents, partially to help teach, and partially to give a voice to the voiceless. Seemed like a perfect idea for our day and age. So I've decided to start one."

"Don't you have a coven?"

He shakes his head. "Ostensibly, the over-coven is mine. But as the head of the ruling body, I have always abstained from belonging to a single coven itself for political reasons. Wouldn't want anyone to get more sway by dint of my membership. But that means I can start one of my own. And I can start an under coven, which will not upset the delicate balance of the system, but will give those without voices a rather powerful one to speak on their behalf."

"And you want me in this under coven?"

He laughs. "AJ, I want you to *run* the under coven. I will be the leader on paper only. A silent partner, if you will. I want to start this under coven and let you run it as you see fit. You wouldn't get a seat on the over-coven council, but there would be some of the normal coven perks. Including access to the libraries and collections of the members." He leans forward, as if he doesn't want anyone to hear us. Not that there's anyone else here. We're in my dream. "Even the silent ones."

Now that is one hell of an offer. I'm not much of a scholar, but the idea of being able to see Kenzel's private collection of magical shit is pretty damned enticing. People with magic tend to make cool stuff, mostly because it will still work even when they're exhausted or otherwise wiped out.

"Who else do you expect to be in this under coven? You need six just to register. Or can you get past that rule too?"

"The young woman involved in the spell, Marcy. She is heading towards the Threshold, and given what she has already done, I'd like to keep an eye on her. There's also your friend Dave."

"He's a necromancer."

"I'm not sure that's a bad thing," he says. "He has less power personally, but might have more of an understanding for how to be responsible with magic. Which makes him a good addition. There are probably a few others close to the edge of the Threshold. Shouldn't be hard to find two more."

"But why me?"

"Because you deserve it," he says. "You've done a great service to us all, more so than most realize. The rewards can't be monetary, and for the most part can't be all that public. You are... less than popular among the community."

I shrug. "They're just mad because I'm the law."

"That happens often enough," he says. "It's part of the sacrifice you make. A sacrifice that I at least believe deserves recognition. I know that the agency does not pay you well, and I know that I cannot pay you well, not with money. But I can at least make your life easier in some ways, I should hope."

"Easier is good," I say. "I like easier." Plus, it would be nice to not have people judge me so much based on what sorority I'm part of. "Do I get a different title?"

"Than Neophyte? Absolutely. Initiate, at the very least."

It's not Adept, but it's a step in the right direction.

"More importantly," he says, "We can probably get you into a more official coven after some time has passed, provided you behave."

There's the catch.

Provided I behave.

INTERLUDE TWENTY-FOUR

Anyway, Vanessa and I only knew each other for about a month when she asked if she could kiss me. I hadn't thought about it. Hadn't considered a relationship with a woman. But when she asked, I didn't want to say no. So I said she could.

We moved slowly. She knew I had no experience with women, and was kind and gentle with me. Mostly, we just signed at each other. Which eventually became very dirty. There's a certain thrill you get signing sexual deviancies to each other across the room during class.

I never let her bring me to orgasm. I did it for her a few times, but then she wasn't likely to literally explode when she went over the edge. I was still afraid I would. She didn't seem to mind, not really. I was very attentive. I didn't think she cared.

I was wrong.

We'd been dating for about two months when she told me that it bothered her. She said that she felt like I was holding back, like I wouldn't let her in. She said it wasn't fair to her. She wanted to know what was going on.

I told her the story of Geoff. She didn't believe me at first, but when I stuck my hand in boiling water without flinching, she started to understand. Then I punched a concrete wall for her, and she began believing me.

But that magic was bound, right? That's what she kept insisting. I didn't have the magic to explode anymore. It was bound inside me. There wouldn't be a repeat. She kept trying to convince me.

CHAPTER TWENTY-FIVE

Unfortunately, being in an under coven doesn't come with a secret club house or anything. I don't know what we're going to do if we get pledges. Do the covens actually haze their pledges? I know I keep saying they're basically sororities, but I've never actually cared enough to find out *how* similar they are.

We're not meeting at a fancy club house. Or even a fancy club. We're meeting at a fancy Perkins. By which I mean we're meeting at a Perkins that is in every way identical to every other Perkins everywhere else in the world. Same bland color scheme, same ugly wallpaper, same inoffensive and uninteresting art on the walls.

I got here first, which wasn't an accident. I wanted to make sure I got us the big round booth, and I wanted to make sure I was seated in the middle of it. It's not great defensively; the table is bolted to the floor and I have to slide either way to get out. I'm pretty easily boxed in here. But it's in the corner, and I can see who comes in when. I can scope out my new magical best friends as they show up, and can see if anyone or anything else is watching us as we go.

The coffee here is crap, but it's the same crap it is at every

Perkins. So I can't complain too much. But that doesn't mean I have to like it.

After me, the first to arrive is actually Marcy. She's still tall and thin, still looks like the walking definition of Goth from the nineties. Someday, her metabolism will catch up with her and she'll fill out like a normal human girl. Or she'll start doing heroin and keep the figure she has now. I'm pretty sure she's got half a foot of height on me, but I bet I outweigh her by at least ten pounds. A younger AJ would have sulked at that. But I don't want to be a twig.

She gives me a much warmer smile than the last time we met, and she looks like she got her first good night's sleep in months. "AJ, right?" she asks, standing next to the table and strangling the straps of a little black purse that doesn't quite fit with the rest of her aesthetic. I wonder if it was Michelle's.

"Yeah," I say. "That's me. And you're Marcy. Sit down. Want some coffee?"

She slides in next to me, not quite close enough to touch, but closer than I honestly expected her to get. She ignores the noise that the booth cushion makes. Except for the inner twelve-year-old we all have, so do I.

"I wanted to say thank you," she says. "Not just for this. For, um, everything."

I smile at her, noticing that she's wearing a cross that I wore for a few days while Michelle was hanging out with me. I move the hair away from my septagram, but there's no Michelle to be seen. Her ghost is gone. "She moved on, then?"

Marcy nods, smiling with a tear in her eye. "So is this the part where you threaten me not to take such stupid risks again?"

"What?"

"I know who you are," she says, puffing herself up like—well, like a teenager trying to look more like an adult. "I've heard about you, about what you do. Your job, all that stuff. Aren't you here to yell at me and stuff?"

I shake my head. "Nothing I could say or do would be a more effective lesson than the one you've already learned," I say. "Besides, I'm not here in that capacity. I'm here for our coven meeting."

Her eyes sparkle a bit at that. "Did you say coven? I didn't think I was going to be able to join a coven for a while yet, if at all."

"Technically," I say, looking past her and giving a wave to Dave. He spots us and heads over to join us. "We're what's called an under coven. Not quite the full deal. More like a training step. At least, that's how it was explained to me."

"Why do you need a training step?" she asks. "I've heard what—I've heard stories."

Dave smiles at Marcy, starting to check her out and then seeming to realize just how young she really is, and sits down on the other end of the booth. He's wearing a button down shirt and khakis, as preppy as Marcy is goth. I feel like we've got the makings of a nineties sitcom.

"I'm Dave," he says by way of greeting.

"Marcy. And this is AJ."

Dave smiles as if needing the introduction. Very polite. He doesn't ask why we're here, and a strange silence settles down over us.

I don't know the other two. Dave is the only guy in the coven, which is understandable. I don't know why women are more likely to get involved in witchcraft; it's not linked to gender in any way that I know of. It just seems like guys tend to go other routes. Like necromancy, which is mostly men. Which explains Dave. There's a sexist comment and a joke about stiffs and erections in there somewhere, but I don't have the time to really dig it all out.

The first of the two to join us is easily the oldest of us all. She looks like she's around fifty, almost a Suzy Homemaker type, but her hair is a light shade of green and I can see at least two tattoos sticking out of her cardigan. I like her instantly.

The other one I'm not so sure about. She looks twelve. I mean, she's not; she drove herself here, so she's at least sixteen, but I'd be surprised if she was any older than that. She looks like she should be a cheerleader. At least she and Marcy don't start hissing at each other or something. Maybe they go to different schools. But she's very peppy. Very excited to be there.

"Apparently, I was the only one who didn't get the memo," Marcy says. The older woman, Julie, and the tween pep squad member Tiffani (yes, with an i. I hate her parents.) both knew this was a coven meeting of sorts. But no one seems to understand what under coven really means.

So I guess it's up to me.

I take a deep breath. "Okay," I tell them. "So we're an under coven, which means we're not a full coven. We're like a training group, or a test group, or something like that. You two," I gesture to Tiffani and Julie, "are here because your talents are pretty close to the Threshold level, but not quite tipping over. Marcy is here for... pretty much the same reason. As for Davie—"

"Dave," he says, sounding annoyed. "I'm here because the witches are trying to decide if they want to accept necromancers into the system and treat us like real people, instead of creepy dabblers in the dark arts."

"You're a necromancer?" Tiffani asks. There's a beat where I worry that she's about to say something really offensive. Then her smile somehow gets wider. "That is so cool! So you like, do things with dead bodies and stuff?"

Marcy laughs quietly. I think she got the same inner-twelve-year-old image I got.

"I don't do things with dead bodies," Dave assures her. "But I do siphon the energy of life to power my magic."

"It's a way to do a lot more with a lot less," Julie says. "I'd probably give it a shot myself, but the idea of it... just doesn't sit well with me." She gives Dave an apologetic smile. "Not that I'm judging you for your choices. Sorry, didn't mean for it to sound that way."

Dave waves her away. He's faced a lot worse. There are all kinds of prejudice against necromancers; he's used to it.

"Okay," Marcy says. "So we know why the four of us are here. Why are *you* here? And who's the sixth member?"

Oh, so she does know a bit about covens. "Our sixth member, the head of our coven, is Kenzel."

There's no reaction to the name from Marcy. Or from Julie. Dave needs to pick his jaw off the floor, and Tiffani's eyes get wide and star struck. "You mean, like, *the* Kenzel? He's our coven leader? What would he want us for? Does he see, like, potential in us or something? Oh my god, are we going to get to meet him?"

I can't help but smile at Tiffani. Maybe because smiling makes it harder to strangle her somehow. "Yes," I say. "That Kenzel. He's the head of the over-coven. He created this coven as an experiment, like I said. He asked me to join because he wants me to be able to join a coven, and none of the others will have me." That came out more bitter than I intended, but less bitter than I expected.

"Why not?" Tiffani, mistress of tact, asks. "You're all badass and just thrumming with magic. It's almost giving me a headache." She then blushes. "Sorry, I hear magic instead of seeing it. I know that's weird. But it's like a beat, you know? Yours is really heavy on the bass, thrumming like some hardcore industrial." She looks over at Marcy. "Yours is more flowy and ethereal, like Enya or something." Marcy makes an offended face. No one wants to be Enya.

"What am I?" Julie asks.

"You sound like classic rock." Then she looks at Dave. "And he sounds like light classical music. But it's hard to hear you guys over AJ."

"My magic is bound inside me," I tell her. "So I don't register past the Threshold on the existing tests."

"How is it bound?"

I show her my hands and my bare arms, letting her see the ink that spreads and interacts with almost all of my visible skin. "I'd tell you to look closely at it, but I don't know if the sound thing will work that way."

She giggles. "They're like speakers!" she says. "That's so cool."

It's hard not to like this girl. But I may give it a try anyway.

"So does Kenzel think he can push us across the Threshold?" Dave asks. "Because I'm nowhere near it on my own."

"I don't think that's the point," I say. "I think there's something else he has in mind, but I'm not sure of the details. My guess is he wants you here to represent the necromancers and bring them into the fold. Marcy and Tiffani can probably get pushed over the Threshold, and—"

Julie smiles. "If I was going to cross it, I would have by now," she says. "But I can always learn a bit more. Maybe what I lack in raw power I can make up for in finesse."

"And maybe there will be a new Threshold test," Marcy says. "Maybe that's the whole point."

I shrug. I honestly don't know. For all I know, Kenzel wants me to keep an eye on these four in case they go bad, and he just isn't telling me. Maybe he thinks I'll be a good influence on them. Or they'll be a good influence on me. I don't know. All I know is that we're here, we're in this together, and we have a benefactor who can show us some pretty amazing shit.

"So, do we get to name our coven?" Tiffani asks. "Or are we stuck with 'under coven'?"

"Mongooses," Dave says with a smirk. "That's a cool team name." Ah, Futurama. Where would stoners in the world be if not for cartoons?

No one else seems to get the joke. Wait, no, Julie does. Good for her.

"I don't know," I say. "I honestly know about as much about

under covens as you guys do. I think the best thing we can do at this point is figure out what we want. What do we want to learn, what should our goals be, that kind of thing."

"I want to cross the Threshold," Tiffani says. "And fast."

"I want better control," Marcy says.

"What do you want, AJ?" Dave asks, folding his hands on the table in front of him.

I look down at the cup of swill in front of me. This is going to be a long night.

"I want better coffee."

FINAL INTERLUDE

In the end, it happened because I let her get me drunk. We both knew what was going on, and knew that I had to be willing to relax enough. We knew that drinking was the only way we had available. Pot is lovely, but tended to make me sleepy rather than horny. So we were stuck with alcohol.

It worked, eventually. And I didn't explode. Didn't kill her. Didn't do anything but have a really good time. But even though I didn't explode, something *was* destroyed. Us.

The orgasm I had with Vanessa wasn't as good as the one I'd had with Geoff. And it had taken so much more to get me there than it ever had before. I realized, and I think she realized too, that the problem was that I just wasn't gay. I mean, I'm at least bisexual, but at the end of the day, I didn't want to be with women forever. And Vanessa did.

We could have kept dating. We were so young; there was nothing stopping us from just enjoying the time we had together. We could have seen if maybe I'd change my mind. There was no need for us to break up. But we did. I'd say it was pleasant, or at least amiable. But it wasn't easy. And it hurt.

Love is like that.

ACKNOWLEDGEMENTS

There is influence in AJ from many urban fantasy writers, and I owe them all a bit of acknowledgement. Parts of AJ were created in direct opposition to Anita Blake or Harry Dresden, but a fair amount of her also comes from Raymond Chandler. He said that a good detective needs to be "the best man in his world, and a good enough man for any world." That was the goal for AJ. Finally, there is something to be said about her origin from Tolkien; she is in a world over her head, and while she does have special things about her, she is not trained to do what the adventure requires of her. Much like the hobbits.

Joe Weinberg has been writing books all his life, but spent most of his time in school. He has a PhD and two Master's degrees, and spent about a decade teaching. But as much as he loves teaching and school in general, writing has always been his first love.

He began reading and writing around the same time, and has never stopped either one. His first book that he read himself was *Conan*, followed quickly by *The Hobbit* and the *Foundation* series.

He writes whatever and whenever possible, producing supplement books for the *Vampire: the Masquerade* and *Werewolf: the Apocalypse* table top game systems, articles for magazines, academic publications, and so many novels. He also works with Mark Rein-Hagen (creator of V:tM and W:tA) on the new project *LostLorn*, where he is both one of the writers and one of the editors.

When not reading or writing, Joe plays table top RPGs, teaches whenever possible, and tries to live with the aspects of his personality that are both fundamental parts of him and parts that he had never put into words before, such as genderfluid and autistic. He lives with his very understanding partner, NicCole, and their slightly less understanding cats, Savvy and Charlie.